A Cowboy's Kiss

A Cowboy's Kiss

A Once Upon a Western Romance

Trish Milburn

TULE
PUBLISHING

CHAPTER ONE

THE HOSPITAL HAD settled into that level of quiet unique to the nighttime hours, the only sounds the occasional beeping of monitors, laughter from a patient's TV, or the squeak of the nurses' rubber-soled shoes on the tiled corridor floors. Dr. Roman McQueen's shoes didn't squeak, instead leaving a dull sound of contact with each of his steps as he followed a familiar path to Room 312.

After a long day of seeing patients at his family practice office, a couple of hours at the free clinic, and hospital rounds, he craved a shower, a good meal and several uninterrupted hours of sleep. But he couldn't leave until he made a final, personal stop, one he'd been making at the end of each day for the past week.

"I bet you thought I'd forgotten about you," he said as he entered the room, a few minutes later than normal.

The patient in the bed, Anna Kenner, didn't respond. She couldn't. At least not yet. But he liked to think that despite her being in a coma, she could hear him. That his nightly visits were helping her slowly navigate her way back to consciousness. She wasn't his patient, but that didn't keep him from checking up on her—just not in his professional capacity. After all, she was from his hometown of Logan Springs, the kind of small town where people did that kind of thing. They'd gone to school together. And for the most part, she was alone. That was the worst thing to be in a hospital.

He sank into the chair next to her bed and opened to the first page of Nevada Barr's *Flashback*. "You ready for Anna Pigeon's next adventure?"

Normally, he read more nonfiction, and when he did read fiction he tended toward medical thrillers instead of mysteries. But Anna's co-workers at the Logan Springs Library, where she was head librarian, said she loved the mystery genre and had become a big fan of Barr's series set in national parks, the protagonist of which shared a first name with Anna. Together, they had figured out how far she'd read on her own, and he'd picked up from there.

He'd been surprised how much he enjoyed reading *Hunting Season*, set along the Natchez Trace Parkway in Mississippi, despite jumping into the series ten books in. He'd ended up reading longer to her each night than he might have because he got so into the story. So it wasn't any sort of hardship to move on to the next installment of Park Ranger Anna Pigeon's adventures, this time in Dry Tortugas National Park off the coast of Key West, a speck on the globe as different from his Montana home as he could imagine.

Before he began to read, he took a few moments to watch Anna as if his scrutiny might cause her to suddenly wake. But there was no indication of change. She'd been unconscious when she'd been brought in after being discovered in her overturned car off the side of I-90 a couple of miles outside of Livingston. It was a miracle she'd been found when she had with her car resting upside down at the bottom of an embankment and it already dark outside. Only a couple pulling over to switch drivers at exactly the right spot had led to her discovery. No one knew why she'd gone off the road, only that when the ambulance rushed her to the ER she'd been unconscious and covered in blood from where her head had slammed into the driver's side window.

Her friends came to sit with her when they could, but Anna's only family was her grandmother, a patient at the local nursing home. The fact that she seemed so incredibly alone and the thought that she might possibly be aware on some level had led Roman to his nightly visits.

He shifted his gaze down to the page and began to read. He lost himself in the story, not noticing he'd read two entire chapters until the sound of approaching footsteps drew his attention toward the doorway. Lorraine Duncan, the head nurse on the night shift, stood there as if she didn't want to interrupt. Realizing how much time had passed since he'd entered the room, he closed the book and stored it in Anna's nightstand.

"You don't have to stop on my account. Just here to check on Sleeping Beauty."

He couldn't suppress a yawn.

"On second thought," Lorraine said, "I think you need

to catch some Z's of your own."

"That is definitely in my near future."

Lorraine walked into the room and checked Anna's vitals, then smoothed her hair in a motherly gesture. "Poor girl. I keep coming in here hoping I'll see her eyes wide open."

He hoped that as well. She was healing from her injuries, and the initial swelling around her brain was completely gone now. But her body still wasn't getting the message that it was safe to wake up. He realized it was possible that message might never be delivered, but he chose not to believe it. Though he didn't know her all that well despite them having gone to school together since their elementary days and having been in all the advanced classes together in high school, he'd always liked her. And he'd never heard a single bad word about her. By all accounts, she was a sweet, kind-hearted person, if a bit shy, who'd persevered despite some tough breaks in her life. Her being quiet and bookish was what he remembered of her from their years in school. It made perfect sense she'd become a librarian.

"You're a good soul to read to her," Lorraine said.

"Caring for people is what doctors do, even when they aren't our patients."

"And yet I don't see Dr. White or Dr. Mills, who are her doctors, stopping by to read to her after their workdays are over."

"I don't have a family to go home to."

"Neither does Dr. Mills. And that's a damn shame, for

both of you." Lorraine shook her head.

Roman couldn't help but smile. He couldn't imagine any of the other nurses speaking to him or any of the other doctors the way Lorraine did. But then, with the exception of Dr. Denton, who was eighty if he was a day, Lorraine had been here longer than anyone. Roman remembered a younger version of Lorraine coming to check on him when he'd been a patient here as a child.

"Are you flirting with me, Lorraine?"

She laughed. "Honey, I'm too old and tired for a young looker like you. Besides, pretty sure Billy wouldn't take kindly to me trading him in for a newer model."

There were times when Roman didn't feel particularly young, but Lorraine's description made him smile. He stood and gave Anna another glance.

"I'm sure you'll be the first person Dr. Mills calls if anything changes," Lorraine said, referencing his best friend and business partner.

There was hope in Lorraine's voice, but it was tempered by a healthy dose of realism as well, with the knowledge that with every day that passed, everyone at the hospital lost a little more faith that Anna would rejoin the land of the conscious.

"Thanks."

He was at the door when Lorraine spoke again. "Your mom would be so proud of you."

A familiar, sharp pain pierced his middle that his mom couldn't tell him herself what she thought of the man he'd become. Not that she'd never said she was proud of him. She told all her sons that. But he liked to imagine that Lorraine was right, that his mom would approve of how he did his job every day, and of the time he was spending with Anna. He looked over his shoulder.

"I appreciate you saying that."

"Nothing but the truth."

As he walked out of the hospital to his truck, he nixed the idea of driving down to his dad's place in Logan Springs. He needed a good night's sleep before he made the trip to the ranch, even though it was only about twenty miles. As he maneuvered through Livingston's empty streets, his thoughts drifted back to how Lorraine had called Anna Sleeping Beauty. She wasn't wrong. Anna was pretty in that soft, normal way that could escape someone's notice if they weren't paying attention. And the fact that she didn't ever seem to do anything to draw extra attention to herself in high school had caused him to not give her attractiveness much thought. He supposed the same could be said of the years since they'd sat in the same classrooms.

But he could imagine her getting married to some hard-working guy in the future and having a couple of cute little kids who would share their mother's love of books. He pictured them sitting in a big, comfy chair surrounded by their favorites and eating freshly baked cookies Anna had made for them.

But first she had to wake up.

As he pulled into the driveway of his small house not far

from the hospital, he thought that Lorraine and the other nurses would likely read too much into his imagined future for Anna. What they didn't know, what no one knew, was that his imagination often came up with life stories for patients, colleagues, even people he met in passing. It was something he'd started doing to pass the time when he'd had to go to countless doctor appointments and during hospitalizations as a kid. It'd been a way to pass the time and help distract himself from the fact that his body was fighting cancer and worrying that he might not win.

Even though he'd now been cancer-free for more than twenty years and had more than enough to occupy his thoughts, the habit of creating fictional lives for other people hadn't gone away. And since he saw no harm in it, he didn't fight it. Maybe it even helped keep his mind sharp, always a good thing for a doctor.

He turned off the engine and stepped out onto his driveway. As luck would have it, Kailee Upton was walking her pair of golden retrievers past his driveway at exactly that moment. His neighbor was not very good at hiding that she was attracted to him, if she was even trying.

She waved with bubbly enthusiasm. "Hey, Doc. Another long day?"

He mustered a smile that was friendly but not *too* friendly. He didn't want to come across as an ass, but he also didn't intend to give her false hope.

"Hey, Kailee. Last walk of the night?"

"Let's hope so. If I wasn't afraid of something scary coming in from the outside, I'd install a pet door big enough for these two. But my luck, I'd wake up with a bobcat or a bear cub in my kitchen. You'd hear me scream all the way down the street."

He chuckled at the image. "Best to avoid that. Well, have a good night."

As he turned to head inside, she said, "Before you go, can I run something by you?"

He did his best not to sigh. With each passing moment, his fatigue seemed to magnify tenfold.

"Sure," he said as he turned halfway back toward where she and the dogs stood.

"I was thinking about hosting a block party sometime soon. I want to make sure as many people as possible can attend, so I was wondering when would be best for you."

Was this some sort of camouflaged play to spend more time with him, specifically, or did she truly just want to host a gathering for all her neighbors? Truth was he wasn't sure. Yes, Kailee seemed to be interested in him, but she also was a social butterfly who thrived on interactions with other people.

"Get me some dates and I'll see if I can make one of them work." There, an answer that was open and yet non-committal.

If possible, her smile grew bigger. "Great! I'll do that."

One of her dogs started pulling at the leash, so she waved goodbye and disappeared down the sidewalk.

As Roman made his way into his house, he wondered if

he'd made a mistake. Had Kailee read too much into his willingness to try to attend the block party?

Well, there was no taking it back now. He made his way to his refrigerator, but when he realized he'd been standing in front of the open fridge for several seconds without any desire to actually eat anything he closed it and headed for the shower instead.

Cleaner but still tired, he crawled into bed after the shower. It was barely dark outside, but nothing held more appeal than going to sleep. He couldn't help smiling at the memory of how his mom had a devil of a time getting him and his brothers to bed when they were younger. Especially after he'd gotten past his illness and regained his strength, the last thing he'd wanted to do was sleep his life away. He supposed he still felt that way to some extent, working and trying to make the most out of each day until he didn't have any choice but to sleep.

Even after getting comfortable and closing his eyes, though, he didn't immediately succumb to sleep. His thoughts wandered back over his day, finally settling on Anna. He wondered if the authorities were any closer to figuring out why she'd gone off the road, if they'd ever find out. Maybe Anna could shed some light on the reason when she woke up. Because he had to believe she'd wake up. She was too young with too much of her life ahead of her to be trapped in the prison of a coma for the rest of her days.

Roman jerked awake when the phone rang. He was still groggy, still halfway in the dream he'd been having when he reached for his phone. He blinked to bring the bedside clock into focus. The red display read 5:34 a.m. He'd obviously been out cold because it felt as if he hadn't even moved during the seven hours he'd been asleep. He noted the familiar number of Dr. Andrew Mills on the phone's display before bringing it up to his ear.

"Yeah?" he said, still sounding groggy.

"Guess who decided to wake up."

It took him a moment to process the meaning of his best friend's words. But then it clicked.

"I'm on my way."

This Sleeping Beauty hadn't needed a kiss to wake up, only time.

WHY COULDN'T SHE keep her eyes open? She felt as if someone had sewn lead weights to her eyelids. Every time she lifted them, it was harder to keep them open. She wasn't sure, but she thought maybe greater amounts of time passed between blinks than was normal.

Where was she? And why did she feel as if moving her body would take some sort of herculean effort she couldn't muster no matter how hard she tried? She felt...trapped, as if she was being held under water by some invisible force. Panic welled within her and she fought against whatever was keeping her from waking up, from moving.

She jerked when something touched her hand.

"You're okay."

She heard the words as if they'd been spoken on the other side of a wall. But then the thing touching her hand wrapped around it and squeezed gently.

"Can you open your eyes?"

No. Yes. God, she was trying. Her lids fluttered, allowing momentary light to hit her retinas. And it burned as if her eyes had never seen anything but complete darkness.

"Take it slow," the voice said again. A man's voice. One she didn't recognize. Or did she? Maybe it sounded familiar, but she wasn't sure.

Concentrating all of her effort on opening her eyes, she took the voice's advice and slowly lifted her lids though it proved way more difficult than it should. She squinted against the light.

"Turn off the overhead."

In the next moment the brightness lessened to a bearable level. She blinked to try to clear her vision, which was fuzzy around the edges. Gradually, the face of the person holding her hand came into focus. She...knew him. Didn't she? What was his name?

And why did it feel as if her brain function was moving in slow motion? Her gaze drifted slowly away from the man's face to take in her surroundings. They didn't make sense. Lots of tans and whites and other muted colors she couldn't identify. She blinked, again slowly, having to concentrate to reopen her eyes. When they did, they were pointed back at the man. He smiled, and the thought crept into her mind that he looked nice. And…what was the word? Oh yeah, handsome.

She opened her mouth, but nothing came out. And she became aware of how incredibly dry her throat felt, like she'd inhaled all the sand from every desert in the world. A cough took hold of her and then another. She couldn't stop. The man lifted her to a seated position, his other hand placed firmly at the middle of her back. Suddenly, a woman appeared on the opposite side of the bed—Why was she in a bed?—and in the next moment brought a cup of water to Anna's lips.

The first drink caused her to cough again.

"Go slowly, honey," the woman said, also in a soothing voice.

Why was everyone talking to her as if she was a child or something so fragile that too loud of a noise would cause her to crumble?

When she was finally able to drink without coughing, the water felt so incredible. Cold, wet, a balm to a throat that felt raw and unused. She never wanted to stop drinking, but eventually the woman pulled away the cup.

"You don't want to overdo it. You haven't had anything to drink in a while."

"Where…?" What was wrong with her voice? It sounded weak, raspy, as if she hadn't used it in… "Where am I?" Her words came out as a painful whisper, and her eyes for some reason sought those of the man, the familiar.

He helped her lie back as a mechanical buzzing clicked

something in her brain a moment before she realized the sound was the woman—a nurse—raising the back of a hospital bed.

"You're in the hospital in Livingston, but you're okay."

She tried to speak again, swallowed against a throat that had gone completely dry. After another drink, she met the man's eyes, then noticed his white lab coat. A doctor.

"Why?" Voicing the single word tired her, and her eyes closed.

"You were in an accident, and you've been sleeping for a while."

Something about the way the doctor said it scared her, causing her eyes to open again. No, it wasn't how he'd answered her question, but something at the back of her memory made her afraid to go back to sleep, afraid she'd never wake up again.

The panic must have shown on her face because the doctor squeezed her hand as he reclaimed his seat next to the bed just as another doctor stepped into the room. The first doctor nodded toward the new arrival. "This is Dr. Mills. He's been taking care of you. He was here earlier when you initially woke up but continued his morning rounds when you dozed off."

"Hello," Dr. Mills said. "It's good to see you awake again. What do you remember?"

She searched her mind, feeling as if she was lifting boulders to look for clues beneath them. With each one, she became more frustrated.

"It's okay," the first doctor said.

She abandoned her search and looked at him. His name felt as if it was close. "I know you."

He nodded but didn't provide the answer. "It'll come to you."

Why wouldn't he tell her? After all, he'd revealed the other doctor's name. Another cog turned in the wheel of her mind. "How long…?" She swallowed, trying to rid herself of feeling as if her throat was two sheets of sandpaper rubbing together.

"You've been here a bit more than a week."

A jolt went through her. A week? How was that possible? She did not have a week's worth of memories of being in the hospital.

She shook her head on the pillow, and for a moment her vision swam.

"Time is probably messed up for you right now, but that will get better," Dr. Mills said.

"I don't understand."

"You were in an accident that caused a head injury. You've been in a coma since the night you were brought in," he said.

"A coma?" She choked halfway through the second word, but this time it wasn't because of the need for water.

The still nameless doctor nodded when she looked at him. "You had a head injury, but your neurologist lives nearby and it was decided not to move you to a bigger hospital. He decided the amount of swelling you had would likely diminish within a few days. Sometimes the body just needs time to heal itself before it's ready to resume normal function."

She started to lift her arm, to examine her head for the injury, but like every other part of her body it felt as if it weighed a literal ton.

"You'll get your strength back, too," Dr. Mills said, seeming to be able to read her mind. "We'll help you with that."

Despite her determination to stay awake, her eyes started to close. With great effort, she opened them again.

"It may take you a while to stay awake very long, but you'll get there," Dr. Mills said.

"I'm scared."

The doctor she knew but couldn't name placed his other hand over the top of hers, sandwiching hers between the warmth of his. Did doctors normally do things like that? She either couldn't remember or she'd had no idea in the first place.

"You can rest without worrying. Your doctors and nurses will keep a close eye on you."

The warmth of his words matched that of his hands, and that helped her to believe him. As she allowed her eyes to drift closed, she hoped he was telling the truth and she wasn't dropping into a darkness that stole more of her life.

CHAPTER TWO

ANNA DIDN'T KNOW how much time had elapsed since she was last awake. Minutes? Days? Another week? The passage of time felt weird, like she was watching it from outside herself and totally unaware of it at the same time. She scanned the room but this time no one was there. Her door was closed, but she could still hear muted sounds through the thick wood—voices, though not the specific words, footsteps, what sounded like a wheeled cart of some kind.

She shifted her gaze toward the window. Even though she couldn't see anything outside from her vantage point, sunlight poured in.

Her mind still felt as if fog shrouded it, her memories. She remembered a nurse and a doctor. Actually, multiple doctors, several nurses. But the first doctor, the one she thought she knew, had a nice voice, a combination of gentleness and confidence that soothed the raw panic that had threatened to overwhelm her when she'd first awakened in the hospital. Only...that wasn't the first time she'd woken up, was it? According to the doctor who was evidently assigned to her—Dr. Mills, if she was remembering correctly—there had been at least one other time, maybe more. The memories were blurry no matter how many times she blinked her mind's eye.

All except one. Her pulse surged as she suddenly remembered waking up with a tube down her throat. Why hadn't she remembered that the time she woke to the sight of the nice doctor sitting beside her bed? Her head felt as if someone had removed it from her body and shaken it like a snow globe.

That thought rang a bell. Something the doctor had said? Before she could grasp what it might have been, the door opened. A nurse entered, but Anna didn't recognize her.

"Well, hello there," the young blonde said, then smiled as if Anna was a dear friend she hadn't seen in ages. "Good to see you awake."

The nurse started checking Anna's vitals and the monitors on a rolling pole near the head of the bed. Anna focused on the woman's brightly colored scrubs. She realized they had the characters from Winnie the Pooh all over them.

"How are you feeling?"

Anna licked her dry lips and searched for the right word. "Fuzzy."

"That's to be expected, but you're doing really well considering what you've been through."

Anna swallowed, and the nurse must have noticed because suddenly she was lifting the head of Anna's bed and offering her some water. Though the cool wetness felt good, she also noticed that her throat wasn't quite as sore as before.

"How long?" She stumbled over the words as if they were foreign, but she managed to get them out.

"This is your eighth day here."

So she'd seen the first doctor...last night?

Anna must have looked confused because the nurse gave her a sympathetic look.

"Do you remember what happened?"

It felt as if she was stretching a muscle that hadn't been used in a while as she tried to remember what had landed her in this hospital bed. Actually, she supposed she was doing exactly that.

"Accident?"

"Good. That's a positive sign that you remember that."

Anna shook her head slowly.

"You don't remember?"

"Doctor...said."

"Dr. White?"

Anna felt her facial muscles reflect confusion.

The nurse held her hand flat a couple inches above her own head. "So tall? Beard? He's your neurologist."

Anna shook her head slowly on the pillow. "Taller."

"Dr. Mills is the primary care physician assigned to you."

"No, other one." She swallowed again. "Not one of my doctors."

Then why had he been there at all? Were they good friends?

"Oh, Dr. McQueen must have told you soon after you woke up. He and Dr. Mills have a primary care practice together, but since you and Dr. McQueen know each other, Dr. Mills is working with Dr. White on your care."

McQueen. That name sounded familiar.

"Know him," Anna said, echoing a fact the other woman evidently already knew.

"Yeah, he said you two went to school together. Lucky duck." The nurse smiled in a way that telegraphed that she thought Dr. McQueen was good-looking. Anna tried to bring his face up in her memory, but though she couldn't quite do it she got the sense the nurse had made an accurate assessment of his attractiveness.

"He'll actually be by for his afternoon rounds anytime now. You're right. He's not part of your care team, but he's been checking on you since he knows you. Dr. White or Dr. Mills will talk to you soon about how you're feeling and what rehab you might need."

Rehab? Just how damaged was she?

The nurse—Anna could make out her nametag read Brittany now—patted her arm.

"Don't worry. We just want to make sure you're up and about in no time. Your muscles will need to be reminded a bit of what they're supposed to do. And they'll likely want to do occupational therapy to make sure everything is healing correctly from your head injury."

The sound of approaching footsteps caused Brittany to glance toward the door. "See, here's Dr. McQueen now."

Anna turned her head on her pillow to see the face that went with the soothing voice. Another puzzle piece slid into place. Roman McQueen. That was his name.

"Good afternoon," he said as he entered the room. "You look like you're feeling more alert today."

It took her a moment to respond, her mind still focused on the fact she'd remembered his name.

Instead of answering verbally, she nodded.

"She said she feels fuzzy," Brittany told him.

Dr. McQueen smiled at Anna, and it caused warmth to fill her. It was nice considering she suddenly realized she felt as if she'd been trapped somewhere cold for a long time.

"That will gradually clear. Dr. White will be by later to do an assessment."

Anna sighed. Dr. White might very well be a good neurologist, but his bedside manner wasn't what one would call friendly. Or maybe it was just that because Dr. McQueen knew her, she was more comfortable around him.

"How long? Can you do it instead?"

He shook his head. "I'm not a neurologist, not even your primary care physician."

"But you're a doctor."

Her need for some answers, at least some sort of interaction that didn't leave her in this bed with only questions for company, must have shown on her face because in the next moment, he moved close to her side.

"How about I see if Dr. White can come by now?"

"Will you stay?"

"If you want me to." He pulled out a phone and sent a quick text.

Dr. White must have already been in the building because Anna felt as if she'd only taken a few breaths before he came striding in through the doorway. After a perfunctory greeting, he sank onto a stool next to her bed and held up his right index finger as Dr. McQueen stepped away to stand in the corner but still where she could see him.

"Follow my finger with your eyes." Dr. White started moving it slowly side to side, and despite an initial moment of dizziness she was able to track his movements.

"Good. Now let's switch it up a little."

She concentrated as he raised his finger upward then back down past the starting point, and then created diagonal movements.

"How does that feel? Any dizziness? Nausea?"

"A little...when you went faster." She hoped that wasn't a bad sign.

She closed her eyes, hoping to get rid of the sudden sensation that she was lying in a rocking boat.

"You okay?" Dr. McQueen asked.

The rocking settled, so she opened her eyes. "Yeah."

"How about we just talk for a bit?" Dr. White asked, seeming to soften his manner a smidge. Perhaps it was Dr. McQueen's presence in the room that had inspired the small change.

Anna got the feeling there was more to his suggestion, but she gave a slight nod that thankfully didn't cause any further dizziness.

"Let's start with something simple. Can you tell me your

name?"

"Anna."

"Last name?"

"Kenner." That she didn't have to think about the answer felt oddly like an accomplishment.

"Where do you live?"

She opened her mouth, but nothing came out. Panic threatened, but she did her best to rein it in.

"If you can't remember now, it may come in time."

May? She didn't like the sound of that.

"No," she said with more force than she intended. "I know this." She concentrated on the flicker of images in her mind. A small house with purple flowers in the window. Cows. Mountains in the distance. A stack of books. Then the answer arrived in her brain as if it were a passenger on a train pulling into the station.

"Logan Springs. I work at the library."

"Yes, you do."

She shifted her gaze to Dr. McQueen. "And…we know each other."

He nodded. "I was a year ahead of you in school."

Over the next several minutes, Dr. White asked her more questions. She managed to pick up that he was deliberately making them progressively more difficult, though none of them should be hard for a fully functioning adult. She decided it was her turn to do the asking.

"What happened to me? Specifically."

He didn't seem surprised by her question. Did that mean

she was making normal progress in her recovery?

"The cause is unknown, but you were in a car accident in which your car rolled down a steep embankment off the side of the interstate. You suffered some head trauma from where you hit the driver's side window with some force. There was some subsequent swelling around your brain, which we had to relieve. We were able to do that with medication, though that was initially up for debate."

She didn't want to think about what the other possibilities had been. The mere thought of having part of her skull removed threatened to make her sick.

"You were lucky that a couple found you, and then you were brought here," Dr. McQueen said, his tone more comforting and less clinical, more the answer of a friend.

"Do you have any memory of the accident?" Dr. White asked.

She tried to remember, but there was nothing. A big blank where an accident should be. "Sorry, no."

"That's not unusual. The truth is you might never remember it, but keep trying. If someone caused this, anything you remember might help the police. In the meantime, we need to get you moving before your muscles atrophy any further and to make sure your body and brain are communicating correctly." He stood abruptly. "Brittany will help you with that."

And with that, he was gone. And Dr. McQueen moved to follow.

"You're leaving?" She immediately hated how needy she

sounded, but for some reason having Dr. McQueen there gave her some semblance of calm.

"You're in good hands," he said with a nod toward Brittany. "But I can stay for a few minutes if you want."

Brittany moved to Anna's side. It seemed as if she was trying to hide a smile. What was that about?

"Try sitting up on your own," Brittany said.

Anna inhaled a deep breath and wrapped her hands around the railings on the sides of the bed. Pulling herself to a sitting position caused her arms to shake, but she was determined. Still, the amount of strength it took surprised her. If she was this weak after only a few days, how much harder must it be for people who were in comas for longer? Thank God she'd awakened when she did.

"Good job," Brittany said. "I can tell you're going to kick therapy's butt."

She laughed a little at the very thought of kicking anything's butt at the moment.

"And it's good to see a smile, too."

"Okay, release the railings," Brittany said.

Anna did as directed and was surprised by how much her body protested. It wasn't just lack of strength and atrophied muscles, either. For the first time she realized just how sore she was. Deep aches and sharp pains reminded her that she'd been in what sounded like a bad accident.

That meant...

"My car is totaled, isn't it?"

Brittany glanced at Dr. McQueen. Neither of them

seemed surprised by her out-of-the-blue question. Maybe head trauma patients asked crazy, stream-of-consciousness questions all the time.

"Yes, its days of being drivable are over," Dr. McQueen said as he moved around to stand next to Brittany.

The realization caused her to grab the railing again. She didn't make much as a librarian, so having to unexpectedly buy a new car was unwelcome news. She suspected her medical bills would be, too. She had both car and health insurance, but it wasn't top-of-the-line coverage and she seriously doubted the policies would cover everything.

The silver lining? That she'd just been able to remember all those details about her life. But she was also wiped and made to lie back down.

"Oh, no you don't," Brittany said, placing a hand on her shaky arm. "We need to get you out of this bed for a while."

"As much as I like that idea, I don't think I have enough strength."

"You might surprise yourself."

"I promise we won't let you fall," Dr. McQueen said. "Friends don't let friends face plant on hospital floors."

She met his eyes as he said that last part, and her breath caught as she remembered something else—that she'd always thought Roman McQueen was handsome. Really handsome. And way out of her league, not to mention her comfort zone.

And yet she couldn't manage to pull her gaze away. Thankfully, he did instead.

Brittany pulled the blanket and sheet away from Anna's

legs, careful to make sure her hospital gown was covering everything it should.

When Roman extended his hands to Anna, part of her was scared to take them. Maybe he'd attribute her hesitation to being nervous about trying to stand. After all, that wasn't totally without merit.

"All we're going to do is go from the bed to the chair," Brittany said, indicating the recliner in the corner of the room. "You can do that."

Brittany really did sound confident, not just feeding her a line to make her move. And a glance at Roman revealed a smile of encouragement. As a result, she found herself placing her hands in Brittany's, then turning so that her legs hung off the edge of the bed.

"Doing great," Roman said, causing her heart to speed up.

She tried to convince herself that was only a result of her exertion after a week of lying in bed, but she knew that was a lie as soon as the thought formed. She was suddenly nervous around Roman because she was afraid he might somehow be able to read her attraction to him—an attraction she needed to stay firmly hidden. Because there was no way she was acting on it, for a whole host of reasons.

She forced herself to concentrate on her progress, not the man standing perhaps a bit too close for comfort. A shiver went through her when her feet hit the cold tile of the floor.

"Let me get some socks for you," Brittany said. "Don't move."

"No worries there."

"Hospitals aren't known for being warm," Roman said as he hovered, perhaps afraid she might suddenly topple forward.

"That much I do remember."

He smiled, and it was a good thing she was already sitting.

Brittany hurried back into the room and made quick work of putting the socks on Anna's feet. "Better?"

"Much. Thank you."

"All right, let's get this show back on the road. Dr. McQueen, how about you help Anna up and I'll help guide her back into the chair?"

Anna thought she detected a momentary hesitation on his part, but her brain was so addled it was also just as likely she'd imagined it. Especially since in the next moment he extended his hands to her. After her own hesitation, she placed hers in his.

He tightened his grip on her hands. "Ready?"

"As I'm going to be, I guess."

"Just picture yourself as a superhero. This is nothing."

Anna snorted at the very idea of herself as anything approaching a superhero, and was immediately embarrassed by the sound. Something made her look up at Roman in time to see him smile again.

He pulled slightly upward, prompting her to push herself up. Her legs shook so much she gripped Roman's hands to the point she was afraid she'd crush every last bone in them.

She felt her strength waning after only a couple of seconds.

"I'm going...to fall."

"No. You're strong. You can do this. Just take one more step."

She wanted to tell him he was wrong, but that would just prolong the amount of time she had to be on her feet. So she gritted her teeth and concentrated on putting one foot in front of the other. Her legs shook with each step, but she refused to let her knees buckle. The thought of crumpling at Roman's feet, her naked backside escaping the confines of the hospital gown, was beyond horrifying.

By the time her foot bumped into the front of the recliner, she didn't think she'd ever been so tired. It was similar to the time she'd had the flu so bad that she hadn't been able to go back and forth between her bedroom and the bathroom so had finally just slept on the bathroom floor—only this was worse. She honestly didn't know how she'd managed the four steps. They'd felt like a thousand while her feet were encased in concrete blocks. And now she stood there shaking, both cold and hot at the same time.

Then Roman's strength was there, holding her steady as he helped her turn and lower herself into the chair while Brittany placed a hand between Anna's shoulders and made sure the hospital gown stayed closed.

Brittany squeezed Anna's shoulder once she was seated. "I think this gal deserves a cookie."

Roman leaned against the edge of the bed. "How'd that

feel?"

"Like I very nearly ended up on the floor."

"Beyond that?"

She stared at him, an uncharacteristic wave of anger hitting her. Why was he pushing her so much when, as he'd admitted, he wasn't even her doctor? But then something in his expression made her really think about what he was asking. Aside from the stunning fatigue, how *did* she feel?

"Good." No, it was more than that. "Like I just ran a marathon."

He nodded. "Because in some ways you did."

"You did great," Brittany said, giving Anna a reason to look away from what she'd swear was pride on Roman's face. She had to remind herself her brain had been knocked around and thus she couldn't really trust anything she was seeing, not fully.

"Thank you," Anna said to Brittany.

"You're welcome." Brittany pulled the blanket from the bed and spread it over Anna's legs. "You feel up to eating a real meal?"

"You actually have those in hospitals?" Anna asked, trying to be as light and carefree as she could in the current situation.

"They do a pretty good job here, actually. But seeing your sense of humor in action is a good sign."

Was she actually known for her sense of humor? Somehow she didn't think so. Not that she was dour, but she didn't remember being particularly funny either.

"Honestly, I don't know. I'm hungry but also feel as if I might fall asleep at any moment." Wouldn't that be great, waking up from a coma only to fall asleep and smother in instant mashed potatoes?

"Dr. White would like for you to stay awake for a few hours if you can."

A jolt of fear slammed into her middle. "Is something wrong?" She shifted her gaze to Roman. "Am I in danger of slipping back into a coma?" What if she didn't wake up next time?

"No, Dr. White told Dr. Mills that your tests look positive and you're responding well for someone at this stage of recovery. It's just a good idea to start training your body to stay awake for longer periods."

She nodded. "Whatever you say."

He smiled, sending her insides twirling again. "I wish my patients were so agreeable."

"I want to do what's necessary to get out of here quicker."

"It's good to be ambitious but also realistic. You won't go straight from here back home. You need some rehab before you can be on your own."

A sudden parade of dollar signs marched through her mind blasting horns as loud as possible.

"How long?"

"It depends on how quickly you progress. That's something you can discuss with Dr. Mills when he comes by."

She sighed. "Is this not something I could do at home?"

He shook his head. "You really need to be in a facility for a while. You just saw how weak you are, and your doctors need to be certain you'll be safe on your own before they release you."

She did her best to hide her worry, not wanting Roman to feel sorry for her. She'd work as hard as she could to get through the rehab in record time. After she was home, she'd figure out how to pay for everything. After all, she'd been pretty self-sufficient her entire life, she remembered. She'd had no choice.

Anna didn't bother asking if anyone had told her grand-mother about the accident as more pieces of her memory settled into place. Why bother? Most days Helena Kenner didn't even remember Anna existed. Others she was con-vinced Anna was the daughter who'd run away years ago, leaving an infant Anna with Helena.

"Well, I need to get to work, but I'll come by later to see how you're doing. In the meantime, Brittany will see you get something to eat. Someone from rehab will probably come to see you, too."

"If you need anything, just hit the call button," Brittany said. "Whatever you do, don't try to get up by yourself. Falling is the last thing you need right now."

She nodded her understanding as Brittany made for the door and Roman pushed away from the bed.

"Thank you, Dr. McQueen," Anna said.

He stopped his progress toward the door and looked back at her with an amused expression on his face.

"People who have known me since elementary school tend to just use my first name."

"Oh. I...I didn't remember how well we know each other." Even without remembering, she knew it wasn't well. She doubted any head injury would make her forget being close to Roman McQueen.

"Well enough for first names."

Even after he left, she stared at the empty doorway wondering about all the reasons why he could have responded the way he had. She knew she should take the words at face value, but her imagination didn't seem to get the message because it wanted to run completely wild.

CHAPTER THREE

ROMAN FOUGHT AN unusual impatience as he made his way through the rest of his afternoon schedule. Normally, he didn't count the hours until the clinic closed, but today that's exactly what he found himself doing. It felt as if every time he glanced at the clock, only a couple of minutes had crept by.

"You okay, man?"

He looked up from where he was attempting to update some patient notes, not realizing he'd zoned out. Staring back at him was his business partner, Andrew Mills. They'd known each other since being paired up as roommates their freshman year at the University of Washington, an arrangement they'd continued all the way through med school. Afterward, Roman had convinced Andrew to move to Montana and start a practice together. Despite their friendship, Roman had been surprised his friend had given up the city life he'd always known in Seattle for a much different existence in small-town Montana.

"Yeah," Roman finally said. "Just off today for some reason."

"My guess is you're wishing one of my patients was

33

yours. I admit, Anna Kenner's case is more intriguing than the sore throats and arthritic knees coming through here today."

Roman suspected his friend was right. The honest truth was he wished he could spend more time with Anna, and not just because her case was professionally interesting. Despite the fact she hadn't said a word during the week he'd been reading to her at night, he inexplicably felt closer to her, more invested in her recovery.

"If you want to cut out early, I'll take the few patients you have left today."

"I'm going to take you up on that," Roman said, mischief tugging at the edges of his mouth, "because one of them is Tina Fox."

"Oh, hell," Andrew said under his breath. "You owe me. I don't know what you owe me yet, but it's going to be big."

Tina was a middle-aged local who found some reason to come into the clinic at least once a week, and she had no qualms flirting openly with both Roman and Andrew in her obvious bid to snag herself a doctor. She was so over the top about it that she made his neighbor Kailee look like a nun.

"Well, you're a man of your word, so you can't back out now," Roman said as he left his file in the appropriate slot and started walking away backward.

"Paybacks are hell, McQueen."

Roman just laughed as he exited the clinic and started walking the short distance to the hospital.

As he walked in through the ER entrance, he met Parker

Varton, a sheriff's deputy for the county and his brother Wesley's best friend.

"Hey, what brings you here?"

"Your patient."

For a moment, Roman was confused. Then it dawned on him what Parker meant. "Anna Kenner isn't my patient."

"Well, whoever's patient she is, I heard she was awake enough to talk."

"Did she remember anything about the wreck? It's been a blank so far." But memories could resurface out of the blue with head trauma patients.

Parker shook his head. "No, but that wasn't my only reason for talking to her. Someone broke into her house and stole anything easy to pawn for some quick cash."

"You think it's related to the accident?"

"Anything's possible, but my guess is someone took advantage of knowing Anna wasn't home and wasn't coming back anytime soon to help themselves."

Roman cursed under his breath.

"My thoughts exactly." Parker shifted his weight from one foot to the other. "I'm afraid I upset her more than expected. I hope I didn't make a mistake talking to her without someone else present."

"I'm heading that way now, so I'll check on her."

"I'll do my best to catch whoever did this. Wish I could say I couldn't imagine somebody so low as to steal from someone as nice as Anna, but that would be a lie."

Roman supposed he saw that type of behavior all the

time, even in a place as largely rural as Park County.

"Keep me updated, okay?"

"Will do." Parker nodded and headed for the exit.

Roman stood there in the corridor, tamping down his anger. Though Anna was likely upset—as anyone would be—about her home being violated, he suspected her reaction to the news had more to do with what it would cost her to replace what was stolen. When he'd told her about the necessity for rehab earlier, he'd seen the worry in her eyes. He'd seen it before in the expressions of other patients who weren't as fortunate as his family.

He didn't know the particulars of Anna's financial situation, but he doubted she was flush with cash. She worked as a librarian in a small town and was already financially responsible for whatever Medicare didn't cover for her grandmother.

But she didn't need to focus on that now. All her attention needed to be pointed toward getting better. He recognized that was easy for him to say considering that in addition to his income, his family owned one of the biggest ranches in Montana as well as a popular hot springs resort. If he was ever in an accident, he didn't have to worry about spending the rest of his life paying off the medical bills.

One step at a time. Get Anna better. Then get her home. And finally figure out a way to help her with the financial fallout.

When he reached her room, she was still in the chair. But he could tell she'd gotten a shower and a clean gown since he'd left earlier. She was staring at the ceiling as if she might find answers there. Or perhaps a money tree. As he entered the room, she shifted her gaze only slightly.

"I saw Deputy Varton on his way out."

"I remembered him. I guess that's a good sign even though I couldn't tell him anything about the accident."

"It is. I'm sorry about the burglary."

She shrugged. "At least there's still a house to go back to. The rest—they're just things."

On the surface, Anna seemed remarkably Zen about the situation, but he had a lot of experience with reading people. He knew when someone was hiding something. And evidently she'd decided to hide her upset since Parker left the room.

"True, but it sucks nonetheless."

She looked more fully at him. "That it does, but there's no changing what happened so no sense dwelling on it. I'd rather focus on looking forward. It's been my experience that it pays better dividends than dwelling on the past."

Something about the way she said the words made him think she was talking about a lot more than her current situation. But she was right—the best thing for her now was to focus on her future.

"So tell me about your day since I was here." The more she talked, the more he could assess her cognitive function and forward on his observations to Andrew and Dr. White.

"Talked to Jay from rehab, got a shower that was likely the most mortifying moment of my life, watched a little TV, and let's not forget the soup and applesauce lunch."

"Best to start you off with soft foods to see how you do after a week of IV nutrition and a tube down your throat."

"Milkshakes are liquid. I think I'd do just about anything for a chocolate milkshake right now."

"A goal to work toward," he said with a smile, wanting to get her mind off her monetary worries. "We'll put a picture of a big milkshake on the wall, maybe a ladder leading to it, and little star stickers for every step you make in your recovery."

Anna looked at him as if he'd lost his mind…and then burst out laughing.

He felt his smile grow wider, happy he'd been able to give Anna a moment of levity. While he enjoyed his job, the truth was there were days when he didn't find much reason to smile, let alone with a patient. And not even his patient. It felt good, really good. Better, honestly, than he'd felt in quite some time. How odd that he had someone in the hospital, someone he'd known but not well for most of his life, to thank for that.

WHEN ANNA WOKE again, she was so disoriented at first she couldn't even remember her name. She blinked several times, trying to clear the fog that had returned.

"Hey there, sleepyhead."

Anna turned her head and spotted a familiar face. For a

moment, she struggled with a name she should know.

"Paige." Her best friend and co-worker at the library. "How long have you been here?"

"Not long." Paige held up a book. "Just long enough to read one chapter."

Anna eyed the book's title. "Since when did you start reading Nevada Barr?"

"Oh, about thirty minutes ago."

"You know there are several books before that one, right?"

"It was just handy." Paige gestured toward the drawer of the nightstand.

"Weird. Wouldn't have expected there was anything other than a Bible in there."

Paige gestured with the book. "This is what Roman has been reading to you."

"What?" Had her hearing been damaged in the crash as well?

"He asked me to bring something you'd like so he could read to you, help stimulate your brain." Paige paused, and Anna noticed the way her friend swallowed, as if past a lump in her throat. "Help you wake up."

Anna didn't know how to respond. She felt as if she should apologize for worrying Paige, but it wasn't her fault she'd been in a coma. Or was it? The truth was, she didn't know. And that gaping hole in her memory suddenly scared her. What if something had happened to her to cause her to wreck her car? But her doctors would have found it if that was the case, right? Instead of borrowing trouble, she shifted her attention to Paige's revelation about Roman reading to her. That didn't seem like something a physician would do. A rehab person or a therapist maybe, but Roman was neither of those things. Not even her doctor.

"Why would he do that?"

Paige shrugged. "He's a good guy?"

Her friend was probably right. More and more memories were coming back as the hours passed, and what Anna had remembered of Roman was that he was friendly, kind, if always seeming to be a tad preoccupied. She supposed it was difficult for a physician to turn off thoughts about patients when they weren't at work unless they were cold and heartless. And though parts of her memory were still hazy, she knew that Roman was neither of those things.

"Have you remembered anything that happened?" Paige asked, taking the conversation in a different direction.

"About the accident?"

Paige nodded.

"No. It's as if someone carved out the part of my brain that held those memories. The last thing I remember is helping Izzy Marion check out a stack of books at the library."

Paige smiled. "We should give her some sort of award for being our best patron."

"Not a bad idea. If we had a summer reading program for adults, she'd win hands down."

Izzy had moved to the Logan Springs area a couple of

years before and was one of the coolest, most eclectic people Anna had ever met. She lived in an Airstream trailer while she was building herself an off-the-grid cabin, thus why probably half the books she checked out were about self-sustainable living. The other half was a mixture of titles about nature, photography, travel, philosophy, and hiking guides as well as a wide array of fiction. The art she created was as eclectic as the artist.

"How long ago was that?" Anna asked.

"Close to a week before your accident."

Anna noticed how the smile on her friend's face wobbled then fell away.

"What is it?"

Paige took a deep breath. "You scared me half to death. I've never known anyone in a coma. It's something you read about, see in movies, not something your best friend goes through."

"I'm sorry."

Paige shook her head. "Don't apologize. It wasn't as if you chose to put yourself in a coma. But...Anna, it's a miracle you lived."

"How bad was it? I mean, they've told me it was bad, but I don't know exactly what that means."

Paige looked unsure how to answer.

"Just tell me. Nothing you say is going to shove me back into a coma. I saw myself in the mirror already. I know I have a fair amount of blue, purple and yellow blanketing my body at the moment."

Paige hesitated a moment longer then pulled out her phone. She scrolled for a few seconds then extended the phone to Anna.

When she got a good grasp on the phone so she wouldn't drop it, Anna braced herself before looking at the screen. When she did, a shock wave rocketed through her. Paige hadn't exaggerated. Anna was sure dead bodies had been pulled from cars with less damage.

"How am I even alive?" How had she ended up in that smashed piece of metal?

"You are one lucky woman. Honestly, I think you should buy a whole roll of lottery tickets."

Anna snorted a little at her friend's attempt to lighten the mood. Then she examined the photo again, marveling that not only had she come away from the accident alive but with fewer physical injuries than one might expect.

"I honestly don't care how you survived it," Paige said, more serious, "just that you did." She reached over and squeezed Anna's arm.

Anna choked up at the raw emotion in her friend's expression. "I'm okay. And I plan to get out of here and home as soon as I can because, one, I hate the smell of hospitals and, two, I keep thinking about how much more it's costing me with every minute that passes."

"Don't worry about that now. Job one for Anna Kenner is getting better."

Anna told her about everything she'd learned from Rehab Jay, the nurses, the doctors. How Roman had come by several times to check in and say hello.

"I guess if you have to be in the hospital, it's good to have such a hottie for a doctor."

"Roman's not my doctor."

"Even better. No professional conflicts."

Anna shook her head at her friend, choosing to ignore Paige's not-so-subtle hints.

"Who is your doctor if not Dr. McHottie?"

"Dr. White is the neurologist, but Dr. Mills is the general MD."

"Well, he's nothing to sneeze at either. Just think if you'd gotten some crusty old coot who called you 'Doll' or something equally cringe-worthy."

"I'm more concerned about having a competent doctor than having a 'hot' one."

"But you agree he is hot, right?"

"Which one?" Anna asked, trying to avoid answering the question.

"Either, but I was talking about Roman."

Anna didn't know why Paige was asking her such a question when the answer was obvious.

"He's certainly not ugly. You interested in him?" The amount of jealousy that bubbled up inside Anna at that possibility surprised her. Sure, she'd admired Roman's and, honestly, his brothers' looks before. Who wouldn't? They were the epitome of sexy cowboys, and their parents had evidently raised them right because they always said hello and tipped their hats whenever she crossed paths with them.

"No. You're missing the point entirely. You see the man every day, one on one from the sound of it. Might as well take advantage of your current situation, turn a negative into a positive."

Anna just stared at Paige. "I don't think I'm the only one with a head injury."

"I wish you wouldn't say things like that. You're pretty and sweet and smart. You shouldn't be alone."

"I'm just fine on my own." Life was simpler that way. People couldn't disappoint you if you didn't let them get too close.

"All I'm saying is that it couldn't hurt to talk to him, get to know him better."

"Paige, what we tend to talk about is why my brain still feels fuzzy sometimes and how I'm weaker than a newborn kitten. Not exactly romantic." The very idea of any sort of romance between her and Roman McQueen was preposterous. Her grandmother had instilled in her that one did not reach beyond their station. While Anna would admit that sounded like some sort of Regency-era rule, she also knew that if you set realistic goals in life you were less likely to fail. Anna had to look no further than her own mother to see the wisdom in her grandmother's words.

One could stretch in some aspects of life while also being realistic. The trick was finding the right balance.

"Then talk about something else," Paige said.

"What in the world would I have to say of interest?"

Paige leaned back and sighed. "You're a smart woman.

You can figure it out."

Anna really needed to get better so she could go home. There she'd be safe from the temptation to act on the ideas Paige was putting in her head. But down that path lay only disappointment. She'd done her best to put past disappointments behind her, to build a life that made her happy. Sure, in her real life there were none of the thrilling adventures, daring escapades or heights of emotion she so often read about, but fiction was fiction for a reason.

Despite her best efforts to shove Paige's words out of her head, they decided to play on a loop instead even after her friend headed back to Logan Springs. When she couldn't even concentrate on reading, she felt like throwing the book across the room—a very un-Anna-like thing to do.

Instead, she threw herself into her physical therapy, pushing herself even when Jay said she'd done enough.

"What else am I going to do?" she said, doing her best to ignore the shaky fatigue in her legs and the pounding in her head. "Lying in that bed lost its allure about three seconds after I woke up."

"Still, if you overdo it, you'll be sorry. And I don't want to get on Dr. White's bad side. Or that of Dr. Mills. Or Dr. McQueen's, for that matter. Basically anyone with 'Dr.' in front of their name."

"They have a bad side?"

"Dr. White, yes. Dr. Mills, no idea. Dr. McQueen...okay, fair point. He's as nice as they come. But he's also very involved with his patients' care."

"He's not my doctor, so you don't have to worry about that one."

"But I do work with him regarding other patients. Plus, everyone knows you're friends."

She wouldn't go quite that far, though a part of her wished that was why he spent time with her rather than some sort of strange sense of responsibility just because they went to school together. She ought to be thankful, but damn if Paige's words didn't make her want to be more than just an acquaintance, more than the patient of his business partner.

"Maybe you're right. I should sit." She refused to accept that some ill-advised disappointment had robbed her of the last of the strength she'd mustered.

Jay smiled in an understanding way, though he couldn't possibly know the turmoil racing inside her damaged head.

That was it. The accident must have knocked any good sense she had right out of her head.

Jay knelt in front of her once she was seated in the recliner, and she realized he was cute in that bookish, glasses-wearing way that made her think she and he might have more in common than she and Roman ever could. But then she noticed the ring on his left hand. Maybe once again fate was reminding her that happily ever after wasn't something she should be seeking out.

Though she knew the world contained happily married couples, her experience had not once led her to believe that it was in the cards for her. Her grandmother had divorced shortly after Anna's mother was born. Anna's mom didn't even have a husband when she'd had a baby. When she'd been younger, Anna had wondered about her father's identity. But as the years passed, her grandmother had convinced her it was better not to know. She still wondered sometimes, but she'd rather not know than find out he was some sort of class A jerk or mooch on society.

Anna had dated on occasion, but her romantic history wasn't exactly the stuff of legend either. Maybe she just hadn't met the right guy. Or maybe there was no such thing.

"You're doing really well, but you have to guard against going too fast, hurting yourself, and going backward instead of forward," Jay said.

Though common sense told her he was right, frustration gripped her nonetheless. But she nodded that she understood. He patted her quickly on the knee before standing.

"I'll see you tomorrow when I promise to kick your butt—to a point."

That caused her to smile. "I'll hold you to that."

After he left, she leaned her head back and closed her eyes. Just how hard she'd worked caught up to her, and she found herself drifting. She wasn't sure how long she'd been dozing when a new sound caused her to lift her eyelids a fraction. The sight of a new person in her room drew her attention. The man was putting something on the far wall. She opened her eyes all the way and realized the new arrival was Roman. For a wicked moment she allowed her gaze to drink in the rear view of the fine male specimen. How often did she get a chance to watch Roman McQueen without witnesses? Never, that's how often.

She was so caught up in a fantasy of being able to watch him from every angle unseen that she nearly got caught staring at him when he turned around.

"Hey, there," he said. "What do you think?" He gestured to a poster of a ladder on the wall, at the top of which was a drawing of a milkshake.

The sight of a doctor proud of what looked like something that would be on an elementary school classroom's wall caused her to laugh.

"I can't believe you actually did that."

"Of course I did. I'm a man of my word. And because of that," he said as he reached into the pocket of his slacks and pulled out a clear plastic package, "I hear you did well with your rehab today. So you get a gold star."

And as sure as she was sitting there, he pulled a gold star sticker free from the sheet it was on and placed it on the bottom rung of the ladder.

Chapter Four

ANNA'S LAUGHTER AT his antics lifted something within Roman, the tinge of sorrow left in the wake of his mother's death two years before. He didn't consciously think about it, at least not all the time, but he supposed he'd known it was there. He'd gotten on with his life the same as his brothers and dad, but that didn't mean the grief totally went away. Maybe it was because he and his mom had such a special bond forged within the walls of this very hospital and others like it.

But there was something so pure about Anna's laughter that it felt as if the sun was shining on places that had been in shadow for quite some time. Some of those shadows had been there since he was a child. They were the ones he was afraid to expose to light, afraid if he did his cancer would come roaring back.

As a man of science, he knew the thoughts were ridiculous. Thoughts and fears didn't cause cancer. The mutation of cells did, and his annual checkups were always clear. And yet each time he received results, he held his breath until he read the all clear.

"Do you do crazy things like this for your patients?" Anna asked, yanking him back to the present.

"If the situation calls for it." He walked toward her and leaned his hip against the end of her bed. "And a promise is a promise."

She pointed toward the poster. "I plan to get that milkshake sooner than everyone expects."

"I hope you do. Jay tells me you worked hard today, but that he warned you not to overdo it."

She pressed her lips together for a moment before speaking. "He did, but I figure if I don't have anything else to do, I might as well work toward getting better and out of this place."

"What, you don't enjoy my company?" Now what had made him ask that? He should be encouraging her to heal, even if Jay's caution was valid.

"You've been kind and helpful, and I'm thankful for that. But I doubt anyone wants to stay here longer than they have to."

He nodded, remembering how desperately he'd wanted to go home when he'd been a patient here.

"You're right about that. I know from experience."

Anna looked confused, and he wondered if she'd remember his illness when they were kids even if she hadn't sustained a head injury. But then the memory must have clicked into place because her eyes widened.

"I'm so sorry. I totally forgot about—"

He waved off her concern. "It's okay. It was a long time ago."

"Still, I'm sure they're memories you don't want to re-live."

"Yes and no. Having that experience helps me to empa-thize with my patients."

"Is that why you became a doctor?"

"It is. And my mom said she thought I had the disposi-tion for it, more so than a lot of the doctors she'd met throughout her life."

"She was right."

"Thank you. That's nice of you to say."

Anna lowered her gaze for a moment before lifting it back to his. "I'm sorry about your mom's passing. I know that's terribly late, but…"

"No need to apologize. We don't exactly cross paths of-ten."

"True." Anna glanced toward her nightstand, and he no-ticed she'd discovered the book he'd been reading to her. "She was always so nice and loved to chat about books when she'd come into the library."

"She did love to read."

"How about you? I hear you've been reading to me. I…was surprised to hear that."

"It seemed appropriate, you being a librarian. There's still a lot we don't understand about the brain, and I figured it wouldn't hurt even if it didn't help."

Anna clasped her hands together in her lap as if she didn't know what to say. Had he somehow embarrassed her?

"How are you liking the book?" she asked.

"It's good. Honestly, I'm not a big fiction reader, but it sucked me in."

They spent the next several minutes talking about the series, other books they'd both enjoyed, and how Anna had become a fan of mysteries as a child reading a bunch of old Nancy Drew books she'd found in a box in her grandmother's attic.

"They made me sneeze, but I devoured them."

"Is that what led you to want to be a librarian?"

"Probably. I remember after that I would check out however many books I could from both the school and public libraries. I've always liked losing myself in a story."

There was nothing unusual about what she said. After all, lots of people could say the same or no one would sell books. But there was a flicker of something in her eyes before she averted them again that led him to believe there was more to the comment than a simple love of books. But it also felt like too personal of a question. It was strange to have to remind himself that their relationship was tangential at best. They'd been acquaintances for years, but he couldn't say they were actual friends. Though he realized he wouldn't mind that changing. Was it already?

He'd told her he did special things for his patients, and that was true to some extent. He tried to connect with them on more than a clinical level in hopes they would more likely heed his professional directives and suggestions. But he'd never promised any of them a milkshake or read to them while they were in a coma.

"My mom read to me to help pass the time when I was in the hospital." He'd had no plans to share that piece of his past with her, but the truth had tumbled out nonetheless.

Anna smiled. "That sounds like something she'd do. Books have a way of taking our minds off our troubles."

"I bet that's an effective marketing strategy for the library."

"Not one I voice, but admittedly I've directed people toward books I've thought might help them get through certain hard times in their lives."

"Did a librarian do that for you at some point?"

Her eyes widened a fraction at his question.

"I'm sorry. That was too personal." What was up with him?

After a moment's hesitation, she shook her head. "No, it's okay. I guess I shouldn't be surprised by a doctor—a good one—being perceptive."

"More logic than perception. Makes sense that someone like that might have influenced you."

"And yet it wasn't. I sort of found my own way. I don't know if you remember Mrs. Thatcher, the librarian at the public library when we were kids, but she wasn't really one for being...um...helpful."

"Oh, I remember her. I also remember when Mom read the Hansel and Gretel fairy tale to us and Wes was convinced Mrs. Thatcher was the witch in the story."

Anna laughed. "Okay, she was crotchety, but I don't think she ate children."

He lifted a brow. "You never know."

They continued to talk about things they remembered from their growing-up years until he noticed her yawn a couple of times. And her eyes were looking heavy.

"Okay, that's enough for today. Someone needs her rest."

"You'd think after being conked out for a week, I wouldn't need to sleep so much."

"Your body is still healing from the shock of what you went through, and sleep is often the best medicine."

Despite the fact she needed help getting from the chair to the bed, he could feel a new strength in her as she held on to his arm. But she was still taxed for the day, evidenced by how her legs wobbled as they neared the side of the bed. Her grip tightened on his arm.

"I've got you."

When she sank onto the edge of the bed, she looked up at him with gratitude and something else he couldn't pinpoint before she lowered her gaze. And going against the distance he should be keeping, his gaze lowered to her lips. They were so close. Too close.

Startled by his thoughts, he released her and retreated a step. Shifting his gaze away from her, he pulled back the covers and let her heave herself up into the bed and adjust her gown.

"I should have asked Paige to bring me some pajamas. These hospital gowns leave a lot to be desired."

"It does seem like someone with a terrible sense of humor designed them, doesn't it?" Good, go back to the witty banter. Maybe he'd forget the startling moment of attraction that had hit him, one that didn't make a lot of sense because he'd known Anna for years. Not well, true, but one would think if there was going to be an attraction, it would have shown itself a long time ago.

It was just empathy and a realization that behind the quiet, unassuming librarian was a funny, interesting woman. One who happened to be pretty.

When he glanced at her face again, her expression had changed. Gone was any joking about the indignities of hospital attire or even the grim concentration needed to get from point A to point B. In their place was a pinched look of concern.

"Are you in pain?"

She met his gaze. "No. Well, no more than usual. It's just..."

Despite his need to distance himself until his odd feelings went away, he sank onto the edge of her bed, though careful not to touch her.

"What?"

"I'm still afraid to go to sleep. Afraid if I do, I might never wake up again."

"I can't guarantee anything, of course, but based on the evidence I think that's highly unlikely."

She still looked worried, so as he reached for her hand he told himself it was because of his experience as a physician, caregiver, allayer of concerns. But as he wrapped her smaller, cooler hand in his, he wasn't able to ignore the way he liked how the contact felt.

"I'd be more concerned if you'd been in a coma longer, but since waking you've been doing well."

"I'm sorry. I don't mean to be so needy."

"You're not. And don't apologize. You're entitled to your feelings and concerns." And then it hit him that one of the fears she hadn't voiced was one he could remember so vividly, as if his own hospitalization had been only days ago instead of years. The fear of being alone. "How about I stay until you fall asleep?"

She shook her head. "You've already spent so much time with me. I don't want to take up any more."

"I'm not neglecting any patients, if that's what you're worried about. I'm done for the day."

"Then you should go home, get your own rest."

"I'm fine right where I am. Besides, if I were a betting man I'd lay good money on you being asleep inside five minutes."

"Oh, so it's not much of a commitment."

He smiled. "Busted."

Even though she might fall asleep quickly, he still felt awkward sitting in silence holding her hand. So he reached over and picked up the book on the nightstand, opened to the page he'd marked, and began to read.

She was asleep before he finished a single page, but he didn't immediately release her hand. Instead, he looked at how dainty it seemed in his much bigger one. Her skin was so pale and soft compared to the tan and calluses that came from still helping around his family's ranch when he had days off. Before he could think about why he was doing it, he ran his thumb across the back of her hand.

When he shifted his gaze to her face, she looked more relaxed than he'd seen her since she'd awakened from her coma. He resisted the urge to push her hair away from her cheeks, not wanting to wake her. Because the more she rested, the quicker she'd heal. And the quicker she left the hospital, the quicker the unexpected temptation she presented would be gone.

He couldn't quite ignore the hollowing disappointment that settled in his chest at the thought of no longer having his visits with her to look forward to each day. Because he did look forward to them. He just hadn't fully realized it until this moment.

And he had no idea what to do about it. Or if he should.

ANNA GOT THROUGH another day of tests, somewhat more palatable food and rehab by looking forward to seeing Roman. She knew it wasn't wise, but she couldn't seem to help it. Every time she thought about what they might talk about when he arrived, her grandmother's voice intruded, telling her to not be a fool like her mother had been, to use the common sense God gave a goose. Men of means only liked women of lesser means for one thing and one thing only. When they were done, they tossed the woman aside like a used tissue.

But no matter how much her grandmother had hammered that belief into Anna's head, she had trouble imagining Roman treating anyone that way. He was one of the most caring people she'd ever met, a reflection of his mother.

"You're doing great," Jay said as he got her seated back in the recliner she was beginning to hate. "Before long you're not going to need any help at all."

"Amazing what not wanting to look at these four walls again can do."

"Well, you're in luck. You won't have to look at them at all tomorrow."

That statement surprised her. She knew she'd be moving to the rehab facility down the street, but she didn't know when.

"I hadn't heard that. Can't wait to get rid of me, huh?"

"Oh, you're not getting rid of me. I work there, too, and you'll still be stuck with me."

At least she didn't have to start over with a physical therapist she didn't know. Needing help to even walk was frustrating enough, but at least she and Jay had clicked.

"Dr. White signed off on the transfer this morning, so as soon as the staff gets your dismissal paperwork done and arranges for a ride over there, you'll be good to go."

She was surprised Roman hadn't said anything the night before, but maybe he hadn't heard about the results of the scans she'd undergone yesterday morning. Or maybe he hadn't felt it was his place and left it to the professionals in charge of her care. She'd ask him when he arrived for his rounds, which hopefully would happen before she moved.

But when a doctor walked into her room an hour later, it wasn't Roman but rather another attractive young man, her actual assigned physician, Dr. Mills.

"Hello, Ms. Kenner. How are you feeling today?"

"Fine." She glanced toward the empty doorway but quickly shifted her gaze back to Dr. Mills so he wouldn't deduce her thoughts.

But she couldn't help wondering if Roman knew she was moving today, if he would find time to come say goodbye. Or had he figured out how much she enjoyed his visits and why and decided to avoid further contact because he wasn't interested in the same way or feared professional repercussions even though he wasn't her doctor?

Perhaps it was as simple as him being busy at the clinic, and she was inventing scenarios that were pure fiction. Or maybe now that she was out of the danger zone, he was refocusing his energy on his actual patients and not someone with whom he was a casual friend at best. And yet... She sighed, realizing she'd allowed herself to do exactly what her grandmother had always warned her against—letting her expectations outpace reality. Sure, Roman was a nice guy, but that was all. Maybe they'd have an added degree of familiarity when they happened to cross paths from now on, but her imagining them as close friends wasn't realistic.

Their lives were nothing alike despite the fact they shared a hometown.

It likely had just been the boredom and loneliness and, honestly, a level of fear of being in the hospital that had made her latch on to his visits with such mental intensity. Now she was taking one more step toward going home, toward getting back to her nice, normal life.

"Are you okay?"

She looked up to see Dr. Mills watching her. "Yeah."

"You looked a million miles away there for a moment."

"Just happy to be leaving this room behind."

"Understandable. You've made remarkable progress so far."

She had to admit she liked that bit of praise, but a voice in her head whispered that she would have liked it more if Roman had voiced it. She really needed to get back to Logan Springs where she only saw him occasionally. Where she rarely even thought about him. She hated how now she wondered if it was possible to go back to a life in which Roman McQueen hardly ever crossed her mind.

But she had to. Nothing good came of wanting something you couldn't have. Her family was generational evidence of that truth. She'd stretched in certain aspects of her life, the first in her family to get a college degree and have a professional career, but romantic relationships were another story altogether. In that area, it was much easier to believe the words she could still hear in her grandmother's voice. Romance was more dangerous because it involved her heart.

The next couple of hours seemed to crawl by as she waited for the dismissal and transfer, and as she found her heart leaping every time someone approached her door. But Roman didn't show. Despite what she knew to be true, she couldn't help that her heart sank as they wheeled her out of her room late in the afternoon, leaving her ladder poster with its star stickers and cartoon milkshake behind.

With nothing to look forward to once she arrived at the rehab facility but more work, she used the phone in her room to call Paige to tell her about her relocation. She started to ask Paige to bring her laptop the next time she visited, but then she remembered she wasn't supposed to look at screens for long as her brain healed. Not to mention the fact that her laptop was one of the things that had been stolen. The full weight of everything she'd lost—car, phone, laptop, TV and even the nice coffeemaker she'd splurged on last Christmas—pressed down on her, causing tears to pool in her eyes.

"What's wrong?" Paige asked.

"Nothing. Just tired."

"Bull. I don't even have to see you to know something's bothering you."

"I just want this over with and to go home, back to normal."

"You'll get there."

"I want to *be* there."

"I know. This all sucks, but it has to be done."

Paige Hamilton, the voice of reason.

Anna sighed. "I know."

"Has something else upset you?"

Anna bit her lip, wishing she didn't have to reply when tears felt so imminent.

"You didn't get bad news, did you?"

"No, nothing like that." Anna debated how much to tell her friend and decided on a partial truth. "It just hit me how much all this is going to cost. I wish I knew if someone else caused this or if it was my fault. It's frustrating that I might never know. And I guess it doesn't really matter because the end result is the same."

"I know this is hard, and in your position I'd likely be worrying about the same things. But what's done is done, and you're not alone. You have lots of people who love you, who are willing to help however we can. I know you're super independent, but you're going to have to accept some help whether you like it or not."

Anna thought Paige was stretching the whole "lots of people love you" thing a good bit, but she wasn't going to argue with the person who probably cared for her more than anyone else on the planet.

"I'm working both jobs tomorrow, but I'll come up and see you in between."

"You don't need to do that. I'm fine."

"You don't sound fine."

"Just a bout of self-pity. All I need is a good night's sleep."

Anna suspected she was lying to herself, but she hoped Paige couldn't hear that in her voice. Maybe if she told herself this sense of loss was temporary enough times, she'd wake up tomorrow and it would be true.

CHAPTER FIVE

ROMAN WAS FINISHING up his half day of work on Saturday by doing rounds at the hospital when he stepped across the doorway into what had been Anna's room before he remembered she wasn't there anymore. He supposed he'd spent so much time in this room over the past couple of weeks that it had become second nature.

He had no idea how many patients—his and those of other physicians—he'd seen come and go from this hospital since he'd started working in Livingston, but the odd sense of loss at having someone get better enough to leave was new. And the strange feelings he'd started having around Anna had been what had led him to take the coward's way out by deliberately not visiting her the day before. Even though he hadn't once visited her in his professional capacity, he didn't want there to be even a hint of impropriety. Though he had to admit that not a single person had indicated they thought anything of the sort was going on. In fact, everyone seemed to accept at face value that he was simply keeping an injured friend company.

Maybe his new avoidance of Anna didn't really have anything to do with a fear of accusations of impropriety at all.

Roman tried to justify disappearing on her by telling himself that it wasn't as if he'd never see Anna again. She'd have follow-up appointments with Andrew, after all. But he'd needed a bit of distance to remind himself that she was in a vulnerable position and he couldn't take advantage of that, even unconsciously. And even though he might spend more time with patients than some doctors, even some who weren't his, there were lines one did not cross. And he'd felt himself inexplicably tipping over it. Best to retreat while he could.

After checking in with his final two patients, he headed toward the exit.

"Hey, Dr. McQueen."

He looked over to see Bella, a member of the housekeeping staff who also happened to be one of his patients.

"Hello, Bella. How are you?"

"Doing well, thank you. Listen, when I was cleaning Anna's room, I found a couple of things that got left behind. I was wondering if you might be able to get them to her since you two are friends."

The rational part of him urged him to tell Bella to just have the hospital mail the items to Anna's address or have someone run them over to the rehab facility. But then he realized he was being ridiculous. Since everyone was aware they knew each other, it wouldn't seem odd for him to check up on her after her transfer.

"Sure."

Bella disappeared into the janitor's closet for a few seconds before reemerging with the mystery novel and the ladder poster. The sight of those two things struck him in the middle. Both had been attempts to help her get better, actions he felt his mom would have been proud of, and because of a bit of unexpected attraction he'd abandoned that mission. That didn't speak highly of him.

He accepted the book and poster. "Thanks. I'll see she gets them."

Bella patted his arm. "She's lucky she has you as a friend."

The praise caught him off guard. "That's nice of you to say."

"Nothing but the truth," she said as she smiled and headed down the corridor with her cleaning cart. "Nothing but the truth."

Roman was due at his dad's house later for a family barbecue, but he had time to make the delivery he'd promised. When he walked into the rehab facility, however, the look on Jay Eaton's face when he saw Roman sent a jolt of worry through him.

"What's wrong?"

"I'm not sure." Jay motioned for him to follow him out of the entryway and out of earshot of the handful of people there. "Something changed with Anna since I saw her before the transfer from the hospital. I mean, she did her rehab, pushed herself as she's been doing, but her mind seemed to be elsewhere. No matter what I said, I couldn't get one smile out of her. She claimed she just had a headache, but I think it's more than that."

"Did you call Dr. Mills or Dr. White about the headache?"

"Dr. Mills came by but didn't seem concerned."

Roman sighed silently in relief.

"I'll go talk to her. I have a couple of things to drop off anyway that she left behind at the hospital."

"Hopefully your visit will help. Honestly, it seemed like her mind was somewhere else. Enough here to do the work but also a good chunk occupied by something that's bothering her."

Though it was likely ascribing too much importance to his presence, he nevertheless wondered about the timing of Anna's mood shift. Was it because he'd avoided seeing her the day before? Or was it simply hitting her that instead of going home, she still had work to do before she could be on her own?

"Thanks for letting me know." He headed toward where Jay indicated Anna's room was located.

He found her sitting in bed writing on one of the free notepads that pharmaceutical reps left at every medical facility they called on. Paige must have visited her because Anna was wearing casual athletic pants and a matching top.

"Writing out all the ways you can break out of this joint?" he asked as he stood in the open doorway.

Anna jumped, obviously unaware of his arrival. Almost as quickly, she flipped the notepad over. She lowered her gaze in the next breath, perhaps realizing how guilty that had made her look.

"No, just making some notes to myself. What are you doing here?"

Jay hadn't been wrong. There was something off about Anna. But his gut told him that he'd get nowhere if he addressed it directly. Instead, he lifted his hands, which held the book and poster.

"I come bearing gifts you left behind."

She nodded toward the book in his right hand. "I'm done with that. I should have had Paige pick it up when she was in town earlier."

"I'll drop it off. I'm headed to Logan Springs after I leave here."

Something flashed across her features so fast he could almost believe he hadn't seen it. Almost. He realized that mentioning Logan Springs had likely just made things worse. It was no secret that Anna wanted to go home. Anyone would in her situation.

"Thanks."

He placed the book on a chair and rolled open the poster. "And we can't forget about this. It's due for another star, too, for completing your first day of rehab here."

"I don't really need that," she said.

"Are you kidding? I poured all my artistic talent into this baby."

When she looked up at him, a hint of the Anna he'd come to know was evident in the crinkle between her brows. She appeared to hesitate, as if trying to decide whether to respond.

"You know that's kind of sad, right?"

"Yes, well aware."

She lowered her gaze again, but not before he saw the hint of a smile trying to appear on her lips.

No, don't think about her lips.

He turned his back toward her as he affixed the accomplishment poster to the wall. "You get one sticker for today's rehab and another for being subjected to my lack of artistic talent."

When he turned around, he let himself slip just slightly into doctor mode, mainly to direct his attention away from the attraction he felt toward Anna. "I hear you've got a headache today."

She made a dismissive motion with her hand. "It's nothing. Just didn't sleep well last night. New bed."

Roman would bet a week's pay that wasn't the entirety of the story, but she also wasn't acting as if the headache was related to her injuries. And Andrew had verified it was nothing to worry about. She likely was just in a down mood.

"You sure that's all?"

She shook her head and didn't seem to suffer any ill effects from doing so. "Seriously, it was just a bad night of sleep."

He didn't believe her, but he didn't think he'd get any more details by pushing.

"Well, hopefully you'll sleep better tonight." A sudden thought occurred to him. "Since I'm going to Logan Springs, is there anything you'd like for me to pick up and bring back for you? More books? Something from your house?"

"I'm good, thanks. Paige brought me some things."

Part of him yearned to ask her if she wanted him to stay, but she honestly didn't seem to be in a chatty frame of mind. Maybe a good night of sleep really would improve her mood and outlook.

Besides, his work had torpedoed family plans too many times. And after the dark period his family had gone through after his mom's death and his dad's subsequent falling apart, things were looking up. His dad had finally gotten himself back on track, and his older brother Justin had fallen stupid in love with the woman Roman fully expected to be his sister-in-law someday. Melody had helped his family heal, so when she said it was time for the family to get together for a meal, he wasn't about to say no.

For a crazy moment, he considered asking Anna if she'd like to go with him. But there were so many reasons why that wasn't a good idea, chief among them being the fact that she was still healing and needed rest more than being dragged to a barbecue with a family she barely knew. Not to mention he wasn't so much of a fool that he couldn't predict how his family would react if he showed up at a family function with a woman, even if she was just someone who needed time away from institutional walls and people in scrubs.

But there was something he could do.

"Can I borrow your pen and a piece of that paper?"

She gave him a curious look before ripping off a piece of paper from the back of the pad and handing it and the pen over to him. He wrote down his cell number and placed the paper and pen on the rolling table she'd been using when he came in.

"If you think of anything you need, call me." He paused, considering his next words before deciding he was worrying for no reason. If he ended up closer to Anna than he did to most patients who came through the hospital, so what? She wasn't his patient, so he wasn't doing anything unethical. "You can also use that number if you just need to talk."

The surprise that registered on her face made him question whether he'd made a mistake with his offer, but it didn't feel like one. He understood the distance many doctors needed between themselves and people who were in need of care, but he'd never been good at that. And if he burned out early because of it, he'd deal with that when the time came. He could always go back to work for the family businesses.

Anna just stared at him, and the more seconds that passed, the more awkward it became. So, he headed for the door.

"I'll check back in and see if I need to add any more stickers," he said, pointing toward the poster on the wall.

He still felt unsettled as he neared Logan Springs forty minutes later, still curious why there had been such a big difference in Anna compared to the previous time he'd seen her. Hopefully, tomorrow she'd be feeling better and he could stop fixating on the why of it.

Before heading to the ranch, he went past the entrance and on into Logan Springs to drop off the book at the library. When he reached the small building in the middle of town, he spotted Paige locking up for the day. He parked and headed toward the book drop built into the side of the building next to the front door.

"She finished it?" Paige asked when she saw the book in his hand.

He nodded. "She said you came to see her this morning."

"Yeah, but I couldn't stay long. Working both jobs today."

He thought for a moment, then remembered seeing her behind the counter of a gift store in downtown Gardiner, the gateway community to Yellowstone National Park that lay to the south of Logan Springs.

Roman started to ask another question then stopped himself.

"What?"

"Did she say anything to you about something being wrong?"

Paige averted her gaze and shifted from one foot to another before returning her attention to him. "I probably shouldn't tell you this—it's not your problem, after all—but she's worried about how much everything is costing. She doesn't tell me everything, but I know her. I know how she thinks even if she tries to hide it."

Even if Anna had insurance, there were still deductibles and things that weren't covered. And she wasn't just dealing with health care costs. She'd lost so much else in the wreck and in the burglary at her house—the perfect storm of bad luck.

"What if we could help her with that?"

"I don't know. You have to understand. Anna may be quiet and reserved, but she's also very independent. She likes to do things for herself. It's how she was raised."

Roman hadn't thought about how it must have been to be raised by Helena Kenner, but it likely hadn't been anything like being raised by his mother. He didn't doubt Helena had provided for Anna's basic needs, but now that he really thought about it he couldn't imagine an abundance of affection flowing from Helena to her granddaughter. Why had he never considered that before?

"Perhaps what she doesn't know won't hurt her."

Paige's eyes widened a fraction. "You know, I like how you think."

After a few more minutes of discussing options, they'd decided to start with donation jars at the library, his family's resort, and the café and bakery his cousins owned in downtown Logan Springs with a promise to get back in touch in a few days to talk about more options.

"A word of warning," Paige said. "If Anna finds out about this, I'm not sure how she'll react."

"We'll deal with that when the time comes."

As he drove up in front of his dad's house a few minutes later, he was still considering options—ones that hopefully wouldn't make things even more tense and awkward between him and Anna.

"You're here," Melody said as he entered through the front door. She walked out from behind the kitchen island to give him a hug. "I thought you were going to stand us up again."

"I suppose even heroic doctors take a break every now and then," Wes said from his perch on the couch.

Roman casually swatted him upside the head as he walked by. "Sorry I'm late. I had to run an errand in town first. Can I help with anything?"

Melody waved him off. "I've got it covered in here, and your dad is playing grill master." She pointed toward the deck area where Roman could see smoke rising from his dad's pride and joy.

Justin came in from that direction, bringing the smell of grilling meat with him. "We're almost ready. Hey, look who decided to join us."

"You all do know I have a job, right?"

"Don't listen to them," Melody said. "I respect what you do."

"You're just saying that so he'll prescribe Redmond's drugs," Wes said from his comfortable-looking perch, referring to the pharmaceutical company Melody's father started, of which she maintained a controlling ownership.

"Careful or you might get a potato to the back of the head," Melody teased.

Wes just shot a mischievous grin her way.

Roman missed not being able to be part of this family

banter more often. But it made more sense for him to live in Livingston, close to his office and the hospital. And honestly, after his mom's passing, he hadn't wanted to be anywhere that reminded him of her. It hurt and it made him angry. After all she'd done to help him through his cancer, he hadn't been able to save her. He hadn't even gotten the chance.

"Roman, you okay?"

He looked up at Melody's question at the same time that his dad and Marty Daniels, the young guy who had been Melody's one-time next-door neighbor and who she'd sort of adopted as a younger brother, came in bearing plates of steaks hot off the grill. "Yeah, fine. Just some long days catching up to me."

Marty deposited the plates he was carrying on the end of the island. "I heard Anna woke up. How is she doing?"

Melody had convinced Marty to give reading a try when he'd had no money to do anything else, and Anna had converted him into a devoted patron of the library. Roman suspected all these women kept taking Marty under their wing because he didn't have anyone else, was estranged from his family for some reason.

"She's in a rehab facility now, getting better every day."

"Has she remembered anything about what happened to her?" his father asked.

Roman shook his head. "She might never recover those memories."

"That's just not right, especially if someone ran her off

the road."

Roman suspected his dad was thinking about how that someone could have been him the previous year when his grief over losing Roman's mom had driven him to make some poor decisions, including drinking too much and getting behind the wheel. Fortunately, no one had been hurt, and a couple of what Melody called "Come to Jesus" meetings later, his dad had left that version of himself firmly in the rearview mirror.

"But she's going to be okay, right?" Marty asked.

"Everything looks good so far. Mainly she just needs to regain more of her strength and the ability to be safely on her own." He shifted his attention to Justin. "I'd like to put a collection jar at the resort for her expenses. Paige is putting up one at the library, and I'm going to ask Lena and Dinah about having them at the café and bakery, too. She'll likely have medical expenses not covered by insurance, not to mention her car and the fact that her house was broken into a few days ago and several things taken."

"I heard about that," Justin said. "And sure, we'll put up something at the front desk."

"Hey, what about the trail ride?"

Melody's question didn't make sense in the context of the conversation, and it must have showed on his face.

"We've been kicking around ideas for where to donate the money we make on the trail ride next month, and I can't think of anyone more deserving than Anna."

Though he wasn't going to be the beneficiary of said

funds, Melody's idea touched him.

"That's a great idea," his dad said.

After Justin looked around the room and saw nods from everyone else, he said, "Sounds good to me."

"Thanks. But maybe don't tell her about this quite yet if you see her. Paige says she's a bit touchy about doing things on her own."

"No doubt where that idea came from," his dad said. "I can't say Helena Kenner wasn't a hard worker, but she's also a hard woman."

"You're the second person to say something similar today."

"Hard not to know a lot about people in a town this size. To her credit, Helena took that girl in when her mother ran off, but I can't imagine growing up in that house was great for a young girl."

And yet Anna seemed like a really sweet person.

"So how did Anna end up so nice if her mom abandoned her and her grandma's a piece of work?" Marty asked, echoing Roman's thoughts.

"Some people are just innately good, no matter what life throws at them," Melody said.

"Is there anything we can do for her now?" Wes asked.

"I don't know." He paused. "Actually, see if you can find out from Parker what was stolen from her house. And I'm guessing if she had a phone, it was destroyed or lost in the wreck."

Wes pulled out his own phone and started texting.

"Redmond has charitable giving in place, so I'd like to help with her medical bills," Melody said. "And if she has any objections to accepting help, let me know. I can talk to her, let her know how much she means to the community and that this is just a well-deserved thank you."

"You're a good person," Roman said. "When is my brother going to marry you?"

Melody and Justin shared a look, and Roman realized what was coming a moment before his big brother smiled.

"Funny you should ask," Melody said, reaching into her pocket. When she lifted her left hand from behind the kitchen island, her ring finger was sporting a nice-size diamond. "Justin asked me last weekend."

"And you said yes?" Wes asked. "Damn, there went my chance."

"Boy, you never had a chance," their dad said.

He was right. The way Justin and Melody looked at each other reminded Roman of the looks of love that he'd seen pass between his parents on too many occasions to count. He hoped Justin and Melody had a long life together. They'd both already been through a lot. They deserved smooth sailing from here on out.

The quiet dissolved into a raucous round of congratulations, hugs and backslaps. Roman pulled Melody into a hug.

"I'm so happy for you both."

Melody hugged him back. "Thank you." She leaned back but didn't release his arms. "I hope you find the same kind of happiness that Justin and I have."

The way his future sister-in-law looked at him made him feel as if she could see more of the conflicted feelings he kept hidden away than he was comfortable with anyone seeing.

"That's sweet of you, but it's hard to find happily ever after when you don't have time to date."

That wasn't strictly true. He could find time for a date if he wanted to, but he just hadn't wanted to. No one had captured his interest enough for him to make the effort, to be willing to set aside his concerns. Actually, he questioned if that was still the case. If nothing else, his unexpected reaction to Anna suggested he needed to get out there and enjoy some female company, if only for an occasional dinner and a movie. There wasn't too much commitment in a casual evening out.

But as he drove home after a few hours with his family celebrating his brother's big news, the person with whom he kept picturing sharing that evening out was none other than the woman sitting in a rehab facility worrying about how she was going to rebuild her life.

And the truth was he wanted to be there to help her with the rebuilding.

Chapter Six

"YOU'RE GOING TO be running the Boston Marathon before you know it."

Anna wiped the sweat from her forehead and shook her head at Jay's assertion despite the fact she felt more of her strength coming back each day. Her cuts and deep bruises were healing, and she wasn't experiencing much dizziness anymore.

"Not a chance. I didn't even like running before I managed to tumble down a hillside and knock my brain loose."

"That's true," Paige said from her seat at the edge of the room where Anna had been going through her rehab routine for the past two hours. "I think she's actually allergic to running."

"I see no point in it if you're not in a hurry or trying to escape a knife-wielding madman."

"Or a herd of zombies," Paige said, referencing one of her favorite genres of fiction.

"I'm pretty sure I could walk fast enough to outpace a herd of zombies."

"Not fast ones."

Anna rolled her eyes. "If there are fast zombies, I'm done

for anyway."

"You and me, both," Jay said as he extended his fist to-ward Anna for a fist bump, a motion they'd fallen into every time she'd reached a new goal.

"When you both fall to the horde, I'm going to take all your usable stuff so I can live a long, long life," Paige said.

"This has to be one of the weirdest conversations I've ever walked in on."

Anna's heart beat a little faster at the sound of Roman's voice. The sight of him threatened to send her heart into overdrive. And then she remembered how rude she'd been to him the last time he'd come by. Not deliberately rude, but she wasn't particularly friendly either. She'd been in a bad headspace. The same problems were still hers to solve, but she'd also given herself a good scolding after he'd left.

"Somehow I suspect you've heard weirder," Paige said.

"If I had, I couldn't tell you."

"Well, you're no fun."

Roman laughed, and Anna found herself wishing she was the one who'd made him laugh. But that really wasn't her thing, was it? She liked to think she was kind, for the most part, friendly, and she was really good at recommending books or helping someone with research—neither of which was likely to make Roman laugh. She often wished she had Paige's easy way with people, the ability to say something witty on the spur of the moment.

"So, how's the patient doing?" Roman asked as he finally turned her way.

"Good." Seriously, all she could manage was a single-word answer?

"Better than good," Jay said, saving her from feeling like an idiot. "In fact, I'm thinking about hiring Anna to crack the whip around here with people who don't want to do their rehab. She's the poster child for doing what she's supposed to."

Wasn't that the truth? When she happened to hear classmates share stories of fun and edgy antics they'd been a part of during high school, she never had anything to contribute. She'd been the ultimate good student, a book-loving nerd who'd seemed destined for precisely the career she currently had. There had been no skipping school, no sneaking into the movie theater without paying, no dates to school dances. In fact, she'd skipped most of them to avoid the horror of being a wallflower and to save the price of admission for college. When she wasn't studying or reading or tutoring—also for college money—her grandmother had plenty of chores for her to do.

She supposed some part of her had lived in fear of doing something that would lead to her grandmother abandoning her, too.

The truth was most people would think her life up to this point was a bit dull and unremarkable. The most exciting thing about her was the fact she'd spent a week in a coma. How depressing was that? She experienced the sudden urge to use this second chance she'd been given to inject some excitement into her life, but she wasn't sure how to even take the first step.

But she had to admit she wouldn't mind if that first step was toward Roman McQueen.

"Well, let's see this miraculous progress," Roman said as he crossed the room.

When faced with taking an actual step, however, she wondered how she was supposed to walk without wobbling with him so close, just on the other side of what she'd jokingly called a gymnast's parallel bars earlier. Jay had responded by telling her that if she could use them to do a parallel bar routine, he'd sign off on her going home today. For a few seconds, she'd been tempted to give it a try despite the fact that she was not in the least bit athletic and would likely end up flat on her ass. Or her face.

But she did need to get out of here as fast as she could, so despite being worn out she marshaled her strength and walked once more the length of the bars, not once having to hold on to them or correct her balance. And because she'd been doing leg exercises in her room when no one was looking, her legs didn't even shake when she spun at the end of the bars to face Roman.

"Impressive," he said. "But you're just trying to make me run out of star stickers."

This time, she was the one to laugh. And it felt so much better than the sour self-pity she'd been wallowing in the last time she'd seen him.

"Well, time to get you back to your room," Jay said.

"I can help her if she needs it," Roman said, sending her

pulse into overdrive again. Afraid he would somehow be able to see that fact in her eyes, she shifted her attention to her best friend.

That was a mistake.

Paige lifted her eyebrows and pressed her lips together to prevent a huge, mischievous grin. Anna had seen that exact expression on her friend's face every time she'd witnessed something at the library that had made her want to laugh at an inappropriate time. Paige glanced toward Roman, then back at Anna.

"Well, I need to hit the road," Paige said.

"I thought you were staying to watch a movie with me."

Paige actually feigned a yawn. It wasn't even dark outside. What was she up to? Anna was afraid she knew and she gave her friend a look that promised retribution just as soon as she was able to dole it out. Paige just grinned and headed for the exit, blowing her a kiss before stepping through the door.

"I guess my work here is done. Thanks for the assist," Jay said as he followed in Paige's tracks.

Was she imagining it or was there a hint of mischief in her physical therapist's expression, too? Everyone had lost their minds!

"I sure can clear out a room," Roman said.

Please don't let him figure out why.

"That probably has more to do with me. I think they're both tired of my face by now."

Roman leaned his forearms against one of the bars.

"Well, guess it's lucky I'm here now to give them a break."

Anna had no idea how to interpret his words. At face value or did they have some deeper meaning?

She mentally smacked herself upside the head. There was nothing remotely romantic going on here, and she should be thankful for that. If she decided to come out of her shell enough to date, common sense told her she should find someone more like her—similar personality, similar background, similar attractiveness level, similar social strata. Roman McQueen fit none of those criteria.

But then Roman offered his arm as if he were some dashing hero about to escort her into a glittering ball like the one his family hosted at the resort each Christmas. She'd seen pictures in the *Grapevine*, what passed for a local newspaper in Logan Springs but was really just a front-and-back newsletter/gossip column. Ladies in beautiful dresses, men in tuxes. It's how she'd imagined prom, another dance she'd skipped. Being an expensive wallflower hadn't made a lot of sense to someone saving up to go to college to improve her lot in life.

She thought about ignoring his offered assistance, but then wondered if doing so would make him wonder why. And she didn't need him examining her reasoning too closely. So she placed her hand gently in the crook of his arm and allowed him to escort her not to a fancy ball but rather her small room. Room twelve was a step up from the hospital, but that wasn't saying much. It was still a medical facility and thus still looked like one. Her house wasn't fancy, but she'd never missed it so much in her life.

Even more than she needed to stop the increasing medical bills, she needed her own bed, familiar surroundings, privacy, and to not worry about how she might react every time Roman walked in the door.

"You really are progressing at an impressive rate," Roman said as they headed down the corridor. "How has your head been feeling? Any more headaches?"

"No. I'm okay. Ready to go home."

"I can tell."

"I doubt that's uncommon."

"You're right about that." He allowed her to go in front of him as they reached her room. "From what I've seen, unless you have a setback you should be released soon—*if* you have someone to help you at home for a while."

He had to know she lived alone since her grandmother had gone to live at the nursing facility, but she wasn't about to say anything that would prolong her stay here.

"I'm sure Paige will help me if I need it."

"But Paige can't be there all the time."

She climbed into her bed and sighed. "I don't need a babysitter. You said yourself I'm doing better than you expected. No more headaches, no dizziness, no nausea."

At least not enough that she was willing to mention them.

"All that is good, but here you have help if you need it. You are monitored. And you're just down the street from the hospital if something goes wrong. None of that is true when you go home."

"I'm aware. But I also know my own body. Rest assured I don't want to do anything to risk my health. But the reality is that the sooner I am able to get home and enjoy an uninterrupted night of sleep, the better. I may dream about beeping monitors and vitals checks in the middle of the night for years to come."

The way he looked at her made her wonder if he suspected there was more to her desire to go home. Of course there was, and her attraction to him was only part of it. But she wasn't going to blurt out that she couldn't stop thinking about how much more she'd owe with each passing hour she stayed in full-time care. She wasn't embarrassed by her life, but that didn't mean she wanted to talk economic stress with a guy who had access to more money in this moment than she likely would in her entire life. When he'd been hospitalized, he hadn't had to worry about how his parents would pay the bills or if they'd be in debt for decades after he was released. She didn't blame him or even resent him for their different experiences, but they were different.

Instead of leaving now that he'd delivered her to her room, Roman sank into the chair next to the wall. "So, what are we watching?"

"You're staying?"

"I heard there was a movie viewing in the offing."

"I can think of a lot more enjoyable places to watch a movie."

"Are you kidding? Here I don't have to pay, don't have

to deal with people talking and have someone to watch with."

"How do you know I don't talk during movies?"

"Well, if you do, there's a pillow handy to smother you."

She snorted at his unexpected response. "Isn't that against the Hippocratic Oath?"

"Minor detail."

She rolled her eyes and picked up the remote. Since it didn't seem as if he was going to leave, best to get a distraction up on the screen as soon as possible. She flipped past sports, reality shows and news even more depressing than her current situation until she found a movie. Unfortunately, it was *The Conjuring.*

"I haven't seen that one," Roman said.

"And you won't be seeing it tonight either."

"Not a fan of horror movies?"

She gave him a "What do you think?" look. "I live alone. I don't watch anything that might give me nightmares."

"But you read books with killers in them."

"Not the same thing. Reading something and seeing the imagery are totally different. So are the horror and mystery genres."

"Point taken." He gestured toward the TV. "Proceed."

She found *Arrival* just starting. "Have you seen this one?"

"No, but I've heard it's good. So you like sci-fi?"

"If it's good. And from my understanding, there is a good bit of mystery in this story as well."

For the first several minutes of the movie, Anna found it hard to concentrate with her thoughts continually drifting to the fact that Roman McQueen was watching a movie with her. And that by kicking up the footrest on the recliner, he was making himself comfortable. Sure, they weren't at the theater or even on a date, but it felt intimate. Then again maybe that was just because she'd had limited intimacy in her life and she was overthinking things.

But as the movie progressed, she found herself drawn into the story, trying to figure out where it was going, intrigued by the plot and by the occasional comment Roman made. When a big reveal was made toward the end, she looked over at him to see she wasn't the only one surprised.

"I didn't see that coming," he said.

"Me neither. But it was good."

"Yeah." He yawned. "I don't see movies that often. I forget how much I like them."

Anna clicked off the TV and lowered the head of her bed enough that she could roll onto her side to face him.

"It sounds like you work a lot."

"I do, but I enjoy it. That's one thing there's never a shortage of—sick people who need to see a doctor."

"What do you do when you're not at your office or the hospital?"

"I still work at the ranch some, and I volunteer at the free clinic here in town."

"So why would you spend a Friday night here if you get so little free time?"

He didn't immediately answer. Honestly, he looked surprised by the question.

"I guess because I live alone, too, and sometimes it's just nice to share an experience with someone else that has nothing to do with work."

"But this does have to do with work, in a way. It's a medical facility and I'm a patient here."

"Yes, but this is more like friends hanging out."

Friends. She could handle that, couldn't she? A little voice told her that wouldn't be as easy as it should be because she'd allowed herself, however briefly, to imagine him as more. But she couldn't sit here and tell him she didn't want to be friends with him because that wasn't true either. Realistically, once she was back home, how often would she see him even if she decided she'd like to try? He'd just told her he had very little free time, and only part of that would be spent in Logan Springs. Before waking up in the hospital, she couldn't remember the last time she'd seen him. She wasn't sure if that was because of her lost memories or because she didn't see him very often.

She realized she'd let too much time elapse without responding. Should she respond now or just give a nod and move on to some other topic of conversation, one that currently escaped her?

"Yeah," she said, feeling so awkward she wanted to literally disappear. Just go poof and cease to exist or at least be transported to the other side of the world, preferably the middle of the Australian Outback where there was no one around to witness her complete lack of interpersonal skills with any remotely good-looking guy.

"Good," Roman said. "Want to watch something else?"

"Sure." Anything was better than her desperate search for something else to say.

The choices were more limited this time, but they settled on *Leap Year*. It was one of her favorites, but Roman hadn't seen it. She didn't know if a romantic movie was a good choice on her part, but the other option was one of those horrible *Saw* movies. That network evidently thought it was October or something.

It ended up not mattering because about half an hour in, during a quiet moment in the movie, she heard light snoring and glanced over at Roman to find he'd fallen asleep. For a second she considered waking him so he could go home, but she stopped herself. The man worked a lot and needed his rest probably more than she did. And though it wasn't a great idea on her part, she couldn't resist the opportunity to watch Roman without him looking back, with no witnesses.

Damn, he was a handsome man. He'd always been good-looking. She remembered having a crush on him in high school. Honestly, she'd crushed on all the McQueen brothers at some point just like every other girl at Logan Springs High School.

In the safety of this moment, she allowed herself to do something she'd never done before—let her gaze wander. It moved from the top of his head, down over his nose, pausing at his lips to wonder what it might be like to have them press against hers, then examining his arms—ones that took care of patients but could also handle the physicality and strength required of ranch work. She imagined him astride a horse, galloping full out across the valley, the snow-capped mountains as a backdrop.

Though lately she'd only seen him dressed in pressed shirts and slacks, she'd seen him attired more like his brothers on occasion. Jeans, boots, western button-down shirt and cowboy hat—the sexiest thing on two legs in or anywhere near Logan Springs.

As he slept, she watched the rise and fall of his chest, wondering what it would feel like to be curled up next to him, her head cradled in the crook of his shoulder, her ear pressed against his chest so that she could hear his heartbeat.

She sighed. Why was she doing this to herself when nothing would likely come of it? She didn't totally buy into her grandmother's class-system type of thinking, but she was also a realist. If Roman had never expressed romantic interest in her in all the years they'd known each other, why would now be any different? Sure, maybe they knew each other a bit better now, but he'd only mentioned being friends. She couldn't pine away for a guy who didn't see her as more. Doing so had destroyed her mother, turning her into a woman who spent her entire adult life trying to get various men to love her to no avail. Anna wouldn't be that type of desperate, yearning creature.

But in the fantasy running in Anna's head, the differences between the lives she and Roman had led so far didn't matter. His seeming desire to just be friends didn't matter. In the safety of her own mind, she could imagine them finding more in common than different. She could picture him wrapping her in his strong arms and pulling her close, telling her she was beautiful and kissing her so deeply he would have to hold her even tighter to keep her from falling.

The fantasy playing in her mind brought a smile to her lips as she soaked in the sight of Roman and drifted toward sleep.

THE SQUEAK OF shoes on a tile floor pulled Roman out of his deep sleep toward being awake. Or was he dreaming about being at the hospital? Because the sound should not be something he'd hear in his house unless he was dreaming about work. When the sound was accompanied by the feeling of not being alone, he jerked awake. It wasn't the familiar view of his bedroom that greeted him, however. Rather, it was the unmistakable sight of medical facility walls...and the barely contained laughter of one Marty Daniels.

"Didn't expect to find you sacked out in here," Marty said, a grin spreading across his face.

Everything came flooding back as sleep gradually receded from Roman's brain. He looked over to see that Anna was still asleep. Instead of worried or nervous, the two emotions he saw most in her expressions, she was relaxed and peaceful.

Despite the unexpected audience, Roman couldn't help smiling. But then he shifted his gaze to Marty and motioned with his head for the younger man to step out into the hall. As quietly as he could, Roman lowered the footrest on the recliner and followed. He resisted the desire to look back at Anna again as he exited her room.

"What are you doing here so early?"

Marty grinned again. "I could ask you the same thing, but it seems like you were here all night."

"We were talking and I must have fallen asleep."

"Obviously."

Marty was loving this, and Roman had no doubt that word of his unconventional sleeping arrangements would be all over Logan Springs by nightfall. No sense fighting it. Doing so would just add fuel to the fire of gossip. Best to stick with the truth—at least the truth that was visible and not the confusing feelings that always got stirred up when he was around Anna.

He still didn't understand how he could suddenly start seeing someone he'd known for years in a different light. Maybe it was just his crazy schedule and proximity combining to create feelings that weren't real. Chances were when Anna went home, things would go back to normal.

But it had been nice to watch a movie with someone else last night. He couldn't remember the last time he'd done that.

Stop thinking about that, especially with Marty staring at you.

94

"So, back to my question."

"Paige asked me to bring some stuff to Anna since I had to come up here to do a delivery for Lottie."

Lottie was the owner of the Second Time Around thrift store in Logan Springs and Marty's boss.

"So where's the stuff?" Roman gestured at Marty's empty hands.

Marty nodded toward Anna's door. "In there."

Just how long had Marty been standing in there snickering?

Roman rubbed a hand over his face. "Since you're here, I'm headed home."

"You don't want to say goodbye to your date?"

"She's not my date. She's a patient."

"You spend the night with all your patients?"

Roman shook his head in frustration, not even trying to explain that Anna wasn't *his* patient. "You've been spending too much time around Lottie."

Marty just laughed at him as Roman headed toward the exit.

Even after he arrived home, he couldn't stop thinking about how peaceful Anna had looked while sleeping. He wished she could be that free of worry when she was awake.

He sank down on the edge of his bed to take off his shoes, but instead he just sat there pondering why he felt so drawn to spend time with Anna. Was it simply that he'd felt how very alone she was and wanted to fill the loneliness like his mother had for him? Did he want to honor his mother's memory by showing extra kindness toward someone who needed it? But neither of those possibilities explained the unexpected bursts of attraction toward Anna. Could he explain that away as well or was it real? And if the latter, what was he supposed to do about it? Should he do anything?

Maybe what he'd said to Anna the night before—that they were friends—should be the extent of it. That seemed like a safer bet, one that didn't risk stepping across a line she hadn't invited him to.

He got to his feet and headed for the shower. Hopefully a few hours of working at the free clinic would refocus his thoughts on the needs of others instead of the flicker of need that threatened to grow inside of him. A need that had lain dormant until a kind librarian had somehow caused it to awaken.

Awaken and demand to be satisfied.

CHAPTER SEVEN

ANNA WOKE TO find a man kicked back in the recliner next to her bed, but it wasn't the one who'd been there the night before. She rubbed the sleep from her eyes, which drew Marty's attention.

"Look who decided to wake up," he said as he put down a book he was reading.

"What are you doing here?"

"Expecting someone else?" He grinned in that mischievous way he had, which told her he'd no doubt seen Roman.

So the previous night hadn't been a dream.

She tried to hide the fact she wasn't answering his question by lifting the head of her bed so she could sit up. In the process she spotted a canvas tote bag on the counter next to the sink.

"What's that?"

Marty stood and crossed the room. "Delivery from Paige." He pulled out a stack of five books.

"Just how long does she think I'm going to be here?"

"I guess she thought you'd have a lot of down time and would need something to fill it. But she didn't count on you having overnight guests."

"Roman came by to see how I was doing and fell asleep."

"I hear he's been checking on you a lot."

She sighed. "Some people call that being kind. Doctors care about people."

"Some more than others."

"I think you've been hanging around Lottie too much." Lottie was a sweet, friendly person, but she definitely had the gift of gab.

"Funny, that's what Roman said."

Oh, Lord, had Marty teased Roman the same way he was her? The wreck hadn't killed her, but she was afraid the embarrassment might. Like Roman said the night before, they were just friends, and honestly new ones at that. She worried that Marty thinking otherwise might actually drive Roman away, kill the budding friendship before it really got started. Just the thought made it feel as if a hole was being carved out of her middle.

And that told her more than anything that she was letting her feelings about Roman grow too much. Definitely time to tap the brakes. Friends did not think about what it would feel like to kiss one another. They didn't imagine curling up next to each other in that recliner and soaking up the other person's warmth, their scent.

"What's that?" she asked, pointing toward a small box he'd pulled from the bag.

"A new phone. Paige, with some help from the sheriff's department, got your carrier to replace the phone you lost in the wreck. And Paige sweet-talked them into giving you the replacement for free."

Anna took the box and lifted the lid. Inside was not only a replacement but an upgraded phone. Once again, connection to the outside world. "If she were here, I'd kiss her."

Marty pointed toward his cheek. "You can kiss me instead."

Anna smiled. Marty sure had come out of his shell since befriending Melody Redmond and starting to work for Lottie at her antique and junk store. She still remembered the first time he'd stepped into the library, looking as lost as if he'd just stepped into a maze. He'd been convinced he wasn't a reader, but over time Anna had helped him to find stories that he actually enjoyed, books such as *Ready Player One* and *Starship Troopers*. They tapped into his love of gaming and the types of stories that played out in a lot of video games. It had given her a great deal of professional satisfaction to pair up a nonreader like Marty with books he'd enjoy. It always did.

As a compromise, she blew Marty a kiss.

"Okay, not what I had in mind. But maybe you're saving your kisses for someone else."

"You are incorrigible."

"Yeah, I'm not sure what that means, but sounds about right. Well, some of us have to get to work, so I'll see ya later."

"Thanks for bringing all this. It was nice to see you."

He nodded and headed for the door. Right as he was about to step out, he stopped and turned back toward her, looking more serious. "I'm glad you woke up."

Gone was the teasing young man only a few years younger than her. In his place was a different Marty who looked as if he might have genuinely worried about her. It was such a surprise that a lump formed in her throat.

"Thank you."

With a final nod he was gone, leaving her alone once more.

She didn't know how many minutes passed as she sat with her eyes closed, allowing herself to fantasize about Roman for a bit longer before she told herself that had to be the end of such thoughts. If others were thinking more was between her and Roman than there actually was, it was time to disabuse them of that notion. And that meant getting better so she could get back to her Roman-McQueen-free life.

So she filled every minute of the rest of the day with all things non-Roman, including her first walk outside to get some fresh air. Chatting about books with a couple of the other patients. Reading the entirety of one of the five books Marty had delivered that morning. It wasn't until night fell and she was flipping through channels on the TV that she started watching the doorway, wondering if Roman would come by. But even her best friend didn't show up every day. She had jobs to work, a life to lead outside these walls. So did Roman.

So did Anna. She just had to get back to it.

She'd just clicked off the TV in favor of starting another

book when movement out of the corner of her eye drew her attention to the open doorway. Her pulse leaped at the sight of Roman despite all the ways she'd tried to forget about him, to shove all the romantic thoughts from her mind.

"Nothing good on tonight?" he asked with a nod to the TV.

She tapped the book on her lap, the latest by C.J. Box. "Nothing better than I'll find in here."

Roman erased the distance between them and looked at the cover of the novel. "Another mystery series?"

She nodded. "About Joe Pickett, a crime-solving game warden."

"It's kind of amazing when I think about all the books and authors out there I've never even heard of."

"'So many books, too little time' is pretty much my life motto."

"You could probably add 'too little time' to the end of anything and be accurate."

"That's true."

Like too little time with this handsome man before he'd be gone from her life again.

Stop it!

"So, how was your day?" he asked as he sank not into the recliner but rather onto the side of her bed, mere inches away from her legs, so close that for a scary moment she forgot how to speak.

"Good. I feel like I'll be able to go home soon." When she'd been outside earlier, a part of her had wanted to take off running. Only she didn't think she was up to running yet. But walking under her own power without assistance was definitely a step in the right direction.

"I'm sure you're right."

"Really?"

He nodded. "I talked to Jay and he feels that another day here, possibly two, and you can be dismissed—under one condition."

Excitement flooded her body. "Name it."

"You have to have help at home. Before you can be totally independent, your caregivers need to be sure a normal routine doesn't have any negative side effects."

The excitement dissipated. "You know I live alone, and I have no relatives in a position to help me. So basically you're saying I have to stay here even longer. Why even dangle the carrot of going home?"

"You have a lot of friends willing to help out if you'll let them."

She shook her head. "You don't know me very well, Dr. McQueen."

"I don't think you know yourself and those around you as well as you think, Miss Kenner."

She crossed her arms. "Yes, I have friends, but no one close enough to take on babysitting duty, except maybe Paige. And I wouldn't ask that of her. She already has two jobs."

"It's not babysitting duty. It's simply someone there to help if you need it. That's all. And it'll still be a little while longer before you're cleared for driving."

"That doesn't change the facts. Listen, I've gotten by on my own for quite some time. I can do it again."

"You're right, I didn't really know you before. Where I always saw a quiet, friendly woman, there's actually a deep vein of stubbornness."

"It's not stubbornness. It's reality."

"Anna, nobody's doing this to make your life harder. Doctors and therapists make recommendations because we care what happens to patients."

"But that's all it is, isn't it, a recommendation? I can't be kept here against my will."

"No, it's not a prison. You can leave against medical advice whenever you want." He paused and held her gaze so long she had to fight her instinct to look away. "I just don't want your determination to reclaim your independence to lead to you ending up back in the hospital."

"I was told my last scans were good. And my other injuries are well on their way to healing. I'm able to get around on my own now."

"Yes, but what happens if you get home and you push yourself too much too fast, you get dizzy, fall and hit your head with no one around to call for help?"

"I'll be careful."

He surprised her by smiling. "I'm sure you will. I mean, I don't think you're going to start a career as a daredevil."

That was true, but she couldn't help how his comment stung. Did he think she was boring? The problem was he might have a valid point. She might go on adventures in books, but those adventures never leaped from the page into her real-world experience. If she ever got out of this place, she might very well do something to change that.

"Fine." She uncrossed her arms and gestured a surrender before letting her hands drop to the top of her blanket.

"Fine, what?" he asked.

"I'll figure something out. I just want to go home." She hated how she suddenly felt on the verge of tears.

In the next moment, Roman did something that sent a jolt through her body so powerful she couldn't hide it. He wrapped one of his hands around one of hers and squeezed. The breath in her lungs seized up.

"It won't be forever. Before you know it, all of this will be a distant memory."

Somehow she doubted that. She would have the bills to remind her. A different car. And the knowledge of what it felt like to have Roman McQueen hold her hand in his.

THOUGH PART OF her didn't truly think it would happen, two days later she was indeed informed she would be going home. Left with no choice, she arranged for Paige to come get her and take her back to Logan Springs. She already felt guilty asking her friend to stay with her for a few days, though Paige had made it sound as if it'd be fun, like a teenage slumber party without the acne and annoying hormones. Anna didn't plan to inconvenience Paige any longer than necessary. The truth was that once she got home, her life would be her own again. There would be no sexy doctors or well-meaning physical therapists always watching her every move.

But she'd decided to allow Paige to stay with her for a few days because Roman's concerns burrowed their way into her mind. What if she did pass out and hit her head? What if in doing so she managed to open a gash that would cause her to bleed out before anyone even missed her? Yes, that was worst-case-scenario thinking, but she had just rolled down a hillside and ended up in a coma for a week. Couldn't get much more worst-case scenario than that—except if she hadn't survived, if she hadn't woken up. She'd survived and come out of the coma, so she didn't really feel like tempting fate to take another go at her.

Though she had her paperwork done, was dressed and packed, ready to leave, she was forced to wait. Paige was still at work at the library and wouldn't be able to come pick her up until she closed for the day. With freedom so tantalizingly close, having to sit in her room and wait was akin to torture. Everything on TV was garbage, and she was having an unusual amount of difficulty concentrating on reading. She was half tempted to start walking toward Logan Springs and let Paige pick her up at whatever point she reached.

She checked the weather on her phone despite the fact she could see the sun shining outside her window. A gorgeous late-spring day awaited her beyond this building. She thought she might never want to go inside again—at least not for a while. She wasn't the most outdoorsy person ever, but there was nothing like being cooped up in medical facilities to make you want to take up long-distance hiking.

"I see you're ready to blow this joint."

She hadn't thought she'd see Roman again before she left, but there he stood in her doorway. If she was being truthful, she was really going to miss seeing him so often, talking about books or watching a movie together, watching as he put those silly stars on her ladder chart.

"I will be happy to never see the inside of a medical facility again as long as I live."

"Well, as promised, I have brought your reward." He brought out his hand from behind his back. He was holding a large, white takeout cup. "One delicious chocolate milkshake."

Her mouth watered at the mere thought of the chocolaty goodness from her favorite local drive-in hitting her taste buds. Her thoughts must have manifested on her face because Roman laughed and handed her the milkshake.

Anna took a sip of the thick treat and closed her eyes to enjoy the sensory experience more fully.

"I don't think I've ever seen someone enjoy a milkshake quite so much."

She opened her eyes to see he'd taken a seat on the bed she'd vacated. "This is the best thing I've had in I can't remember how long. I can't believe you actually brought this."

"Of course I did. I'm a man of my word, and your quick progress deserves a reward. Not everyone tumbles down the side of a hill, cracks her head, is in a coma for a week, looks like she went a few rounds with Pacquiao and strolls out on her own two determined feet less than a month later."

"Thank you."

"You're very welcome."

The open friendliness in his gaze nearly made her melt faster than the milkshake. Why couldn't she have grown up in a normal home with loving parents who didn't teach her to manage expectations? Who instead told her to go after whatever lofty goal she might have—including seeing if anything was possible with the man in front of her. Of course, she could ignore what she'd been taught...

"So, you ready to go?"

"Yeah, but I have to wait for Paige to get off work."

"No, you don't. I'm your chauffeur back to Logan Springs."

"What? It's the middle of the day. Don't you have patients to see?"

"Nope. Dr. Mills is covering today because I'm covering for him next weekend when he flies to Seattle to visit his parents."

"But don't you have something better to do?"

"Are you kidding? What's not to like about a drive down the Paradise Valley on such a beautiful day?"

If she thought spending time with him up until now had been nerve-racking, how was she going to deal with the close proximity of being in the same vehicle?

"I don't want to be an imposition."

"Just stop that," he said. "You're not an imposition. I've been ordered to the ranch anyway. Wedding planning."

Her heart dropped all the way to her feet. "Wedding planning?"

Damn if her voice didn't break. Thankfully, Roman didn't seem to notice.

"Yeah, Justin popped the question."

"Oh, that's wonderful. Please tell them I said congratulations."

"Will do."

Justin McQueen and Melody Redmond looked more in love with each other every time she saw them. She and Paige had both wondered what it would be like to have a man look at them the way Justin looked at Melody, like she was the only woman in the world. Now Anna wondered if she'd ever be able to imagine a guy other than Roman in that role.

"Well, I can enjoy this milkshake just as well, probably more, outside this building." She got to her feet before Roman could offer any help.

Instead, he grabbed the two bags containing her belongings. "Your chariot awaits."

"Why didn't you get a milkshake, too?" she asked as they walked out the exit into the glorious sunshine.

"I did. It didn't last long."

She laughed. "It's not that long of a drive from there to here. Did you give yourself brain freeze?"

"Maybe a little, but it's hard to resist something you want so much."

She knew he was talking about a milkshake, but her skin tingled nonetheless. Truer words had never been spoken. Though she'd told herself over and over that she should let go of the fantasy of being with Roman, she couldn't help imagining for a moment that his words were about her.

"So, why are you helping with the wedding planning?" she asked when they were both in his truck and headed through Livingston. "Isn't that usually the bride and groom's thing?"

"Oh, don't worry. This is definitely the bride's thing, and when Melody Redmond summons one, one goes."

"You make her sound bossy."

"Not bossy, but the woman ran a large company. She's used to commanding the troops, so to speak. But we don't mind—not too much anyway. She's part of the family even if she doesn't bear the name yet."

Something stirred in Anna's middle. What would it be like to be a part of the McQueen family? It wasn't even their money that attracted her. They just seemed so close-knit and happy to be together whenever she saw them out and about. No matter how many movies she watched or books she read in which there were big, happy families, she couldn't quite grasp what that would actually feel like.

Hard to imagine what you'd never had.

"I'm sure it'll be a lovely wedding." Chances were it would be the type of event that got its own magazine spread, even though both Justin and Melody seemed like very down-to-earth people despite the numbers on their bank account balances. Still, there was no denying people of their stature usually had extravagant weddings because everyone went into marriage thinking it would be the only one. About half the time they were right.

Conversation seemed to fall away as soon as they cleared the southern edge of Livingston and drove into the beauty of the Paradise Valley. She sipped the last of her milkshake as she took in the view of the Absaroka and Gallatin mountain ranges at the edges of the valley as if she'd never seen them before. The glint of the sun off the Yellowstone River warmed parts of her that had grown cold while cooped up in first the hospital then the rehab center. She anticipated the sense of freedom flowing through her only increasing as she got closer to Logan Springs and finally back in her own home.

"You're awfully quiet," Roman said.

"You don't realize how much you take normal, everyday life for granted until it's snatched away from you. I think I might actually sleep outside for a week."

He chuckled a little at that, then went quiet again.

"I didn't think to ask if you wanted to stop by to visit your grandmother before we left town."

"No need. She barely ever remembers who I am anymore. And I called to check in after Marty brought me a phone. She hadn't even noticed that I'd not been by."

"I'm sorry."

Anna shrugged. "Just one of those things."

Despite her grandmother not being the softest, most caring person ever, she was still the only family Anna had. Even though Helena was still alive, there were many days when Anna felt as if she'd already lost her only living relative. And yet, just knowing that Helena was still living and breathing, even if she didn't remember Anna, was a tether to family, to not being completely alone in the world.

"I think dementia is one of the cruelest fates anyone can suffer. I wouldn't wish it on anyone," he said.

"I agree. I can't imagine anything worse than knowing you're going to forget the people you care about, will eventually even lose any memory of yourself." She took a breath and stared out her window. "It must be a thousand times worse than how I felt when I woke up from the coma, and that scared me half to death."

"I've seen patients succumb to a lot of different things, but my hope is that I go instantly when the times comes. Anything that is inevitable but makes a person linger is just cosmic cruelty, if you ask me."

Anna looked over at Roman, whose gaze was focused straight ahead on the highway. There was no mistaking he was a strong person, but she sensed he was remembering a time when he hadn't been.

"Were you afraid that would happen to you?" she asked, then thought that was an awfully personal thing to ask someone you weren't closer to than she was to Roman.

"Yeah. On more than one occasion." He glanced over at

her before returning his attention to the road. "If I'm being honest, I still worry about it."

A jolt of concern not for herself went through Anna. "But you're still cancer-free, right? Have been for years?"

"As of my last annual exam, but the thought is always in the back of my mind."

She shifted her eyes to stare at the road disappearing under Roman's truck. "I suppose that's normal once you've gone through something like that."

And it showed that no matter how much money someone had, disease or disaster could strike them just as easily. Maybe she and Roman weren't so different after all.

"Yeah. You live your life and don't dwell on it, but you never forget it."

"Great. I guess I'll be worried about falling into a coma for the rest of my life."

"That's not the same thing. It was the result of a one-time injury. After you fully recover, you should have nothing to worry about. It's not like a disease that can go into remission but come back at some future point."

She wanted to believe him, but the thought of going to sleep and not waking up again was almost as frightening as slowly losing her mind.

Thankfully, their conversation drifted to more inconsequential things than life and death as they drew closer to Logan Springs. When they reached the edge of town, she told him what street she lived on. When he turned onto Valley Avenue, she noticed a series of colorful balloons attached to trees and mailboxes.

"Someone must be having a birthday party," she said.

But then he pulled into her driveway and she saw the large "Welcome Home" banner hanging over her front steps.

She looked over at Roman, wondering if it was possible he'd done this but was unable to voice the question. If he hadn't, she'd feel a fool.

"Don't look at me. This was all Paige." He glanced at the porch. "Speak of the devil."

Anna shifted her gaze toward the house and saw her best friend hurrying down the steps, a wide grin on her face.

"I'm so glad you're home," Paige said when she opened the passenger door of Roman's truck. Anna barely got her feet on the ground before Paige wrapped her arms around her as if she'd been lost at sea for a year.

Like a whirlwind, Paige turned to escort Anna toward the house. Anna glanced over her shoulder to find Roman grinning as he retrieved her things from the back of the truck. It hit her that in a matter of minutes, Roman would drive away from her house, leaving her back with her old life—the one in which he didn't visit her every day. Gone were the days when she could privately look forward to seeing him, talking and laughing with him. She suddenly wanted nothing more than to crawl into bed with a good book and try to reacclimatize to her normal life.

But as soon as she walked through her front door, she knew that wasn't happening anytime soon.

Chapter Eight

ROMAN WAS JUST stepping across the threshold of Anna's house when he heard the people assembled inside call out, "Surprise!" Startled, Anna took a step backward. Instinctively, he dropped everything he was carrying and reached up just as she bumped into him. He gripped her shoulders so that she wouldn't fall. The last thing she needed after the injuries she'd sustained was to fall and hit her head. In that moment, he sort of wanted to wrap her in thick Bubble Wrap.

She quickly stepped out of his grasp. "Sorry."

"No harm."

She shifted her attention back to the people assembled in her living room, and the look on her face made her appear as if she was wondering if the people were really there or a figment of her imagination.

Paige clapped, obviously happy that her surprise was indeed a surprise. Anna scanned the crowd, which included Katie, who also worked at the library, and the library volunteers, several local business owners, including Roman's cousins Lena and Dinah, and even Marty.

"I wasn't expecting this," Anna said.

"That's why it's called a surprise party, silly," Paige said as she wrapped her arm around Anna's and led her toward the kitchen, where a cake from Dinah's bakery sat in the center of the table.

"Paige said your favorite flavor was chocolate," Dinah said as she picked up the cake knife.

"It is."

"Wait, before we cut that gorgeous cake, we need some photos." Paige started arranging people around Anna, who still looked a bit dumbstruck by all the activity.

Roman watched her closely, ready to step in if he thought it was becoming too much for her.

"Come here, Roman," Paige said, waving for him to join everyone else at the other end of the table.

"I can take the photos," he said without moving. From that vantage point, he could watch Anna. He ignored the voice that was telling him the reason why he wanted to was only partially medical in nature.

"Oh, no you don't," Paige said. "You helped get her here. You have to be in the picture."

"You heard the woman," Lena said as she took Paige's phone and waved her cousin toward the gathering behind the cake.

He stepped up to the edge of the crowd, but Paige tugged him toward the middle. Right next to Anna. A sudden awkwardness that this positioning could be interpreted as meaning more than it did crept over him, so he was careful not to touch Anna. He clasped his hands in front of him, picturing himself in his lab coat, professional in every way.

But he wasn't Anna's doctor. He was her friend, right? But if that was the case, why was he suddenly so concerned about touching her?

He told himself he simply didn't want a single person to even think there might be any impropriety. Even though he wasn't officially her physician, he had still spent time with her in the hospital, had checked in on her, had driven her home. Sometimes assumptions spread faster than the truth, especially in small towns.

"You okay, Roman?" Lena asked after taking the first photo. "You look as stiff as a fence post."

Hell, why did she have to point that out?

"Sorry, just making room for everyone."

"Chill. It's not as if I'm trying to fit the entire town in one shot."

He wanted so badly to glance over at Anna, to see if she was reading anything into what Lena had said about his stance. But he kept his gaze forward, loosened his posture and smiled.

After the picture taking was done, he casually gravitated away from Anna, talking instead to his cousins, Marty, Nell Jansen who owned Springs Pizza, and basically anyone who wasn't Anna. But he kept an eye on her as he chatted and ate his piece of cake. When he noticed she was beginning to look tired, slower in her responses and her smiles weaker, he started to call an end to the party. But Paige beat him to it.

"Okay, everyone. Thanks so much for coming to welcome Anna home, but I think our girl needs to get some rest now."

Though she tried to smile and not show it, he could tell Anna was relieved. He'd been conflicted about the welcome home party idea at first, concerned it might be too much too soon, but he'd come around to the idea that it was important for Anna to see she wasn't truly alone. That she had friends and support if she needed it.

He waited until everyone was gone but Paige before he headed for the door. Anna accompanied him.

"Thanks for the ride home. And the milkshake."

"You're welcome. Call if you need anything. You still have my number, right?"

"Yes, but you've done enough already. You can get back to your regularly scheduled life." She smiled, but for some reason it seemed a bit shaky.

He wanted to correct her, to say that nothing he'd done for her was an imposition. But he didn't know exactly what or how he wanted to say it, and he definitely didn't want to do so with an audience. So instead he gave a nod to Paige, a quick smile to Anna, and turned to leave. As he left the balloon-festooned street, an odd sense of loss pressed down on him. He headed to the ranch, hoping to rid himself of the feeling through some hot, sweaty work that had nothing to do with dispensing medical advice.

★

DESPITE A DESIRE to watch Roman as he left, Anna shut the door and turned to clean up the kitchen.

Paige waved her off. "Go sit. I've got this."

"I'm not an invalid, you know."

"No, but you still need to rest. That's more people than you've had to interact with in a while."

"You obviously don't realize how many people come in and out of hospital rooms at all hours."

"That's not the same. And besides, it wasn't all bad. After all, you had the handsome Dr. McQueen visiting regularly."

Anna looked at her friend with suspicion. "Whatever you have up your sleeve, just forget about it. There is nothing between me and Roman."

"But do you want there to be?"

"No."

"If they gave out awards for being terrible liars, you would be the grand champion."

"You don't know what you're talking about."

"Why can't you just admit that you like him?"

"Of course, I like him. He's a nice guy and helped pass some of the endless hours in the hospital."

"Now why would he do that?"

"Um, because he's a nice guy." Anna didn't need Paige putting illogical hopes in her head.

"Does he read to all the patients in the hospital like it's

story time?"

"I have no idea."

"Yes, you do."

"Maybe it's because I was the only one in a flipping coma." Anna pressed her hands to her temples. "I'm going to go lie down for a bit."

Paige's expression changed to one of worry. "Are you okay?"

"I'm fine. It's just a headache, probably from eating so much sugar."

"You only had one piece of cake."

"I'd already had a milkshake earlier." Anna knew she'd made a mistake the moment the words left her mouth.

Paige grinned. "So Roman got you the reward milkshake. I bet he doesn't do that for other patients, either."

Anna sighed and shook her head before turning and heading to her room. But once she'd shut the door behind her and stretched out on the bed, it was weird how strange it felt after so long lying in institutional beds. And the quiet seemed weird, too, broken only by the sounds of Paige moving around in the kitchen and a lawnmower on the next street over.

But this was what she'd wanted, what she'd longed for every day since she'd awakened in the hospital. And yet she felt out of sorts, as if life still wasn't back to normal. Maybe once she got a good night's sleep in her own bed, showered in her own shower with her own shampoo, and made breakfast in her own kitchen, the lingering sense of being a visitor in her own life would disappear.

She must have drifted off because when she woke, the room was dark though she could see a sliver of light shining underneath her bedroom door. Her body felt heavy and for a frightening moment she wondered if she was coming out of another coma. But Dr. White had said that a recurrence was highly unlikely. And he was a neurologist, so he should know, right?

She forced herself to take a few slow, deep breaths before getting out of bed. A glance at the clock told her she'd been asleep for close to five hours, and she felt as if she could sleep five more. But her stomach told her that she needed something more substantial than milkshakes or cake.

After washing her face in the bathroom, she felt marginally more awake as she left the bedroom and headed for the kitchen. Despite the fact that Roman had said she should have someone with her for a while, she was still a little startled to see Paige curled up on one end of the couch reading a new memoir everyone was talking about by an actress who'd grown up homeless on the streets of L.A., but who now was raking in both sizeable paydays and awards.

"I thought that had at least a half dozen holds on it."

"It does, but since we closed early today and it came in this morning, I thought I could sneak in reading it tonight. It's as good as everyone is saying. It's amazing what people can accomplish when they really want something."

Anna felt like there was a not-so-hidden message in Paige's words, but she pretended like she didn't notice and instead headed toward the kitchen.

"I just ordered pizza. Should be here any minute."

"That sounds good."

"I know. It's your go-to comfort food. That and chocolate."

"Ever wonder why comfort food is never a healthy salad?"

"Nope."

Anna laughed as she sank onto the opposite end of the couch. "I didn't mean to sleep so long."

"I'm surprised you didn't sleep longer. I'm sure the whole recovering from a car accident and coma thing is quite tiring. Not to mention hiding how much you like a guy."

"You certainly are persistent."

"Is it working?" Paige grinned in that mischievous way she had.

"How about I just focus on getting back to normality?"

Paige closed the book and waved away Anna's idea. "Who wants normality when they can have excitement?"

"Me. I like my life just the way it was before I for some reason careened down a hillside." She said the words, but she wasn't sure they were totally true. Hadn't she wondered about injecting something new into her life?

"Are you sure about that?"

"Did I do or say anything that indicated I was unhappy?" Sure, she was having thoughts about shaking things up a little, but she didn't know what form that might take and thus wasn't ready to talk about it.

"Well, no, but—"

"Then stop acting like you've done a binge reading of every book in the romance section of the library."

Paige started to reply, but a knock at the door gave Anna an excuse to walk away from the conversation. She opened the front door to find Marty standing there, a large pizza box in his hands.

"Weren't you just here?"

"Hours ago. Looks like one of us took a nap since then." He motioned toward her hair, which she'd evidently not tamed enough during her brief trip to the bathroom, and grinned.

"You know insulting your customers isn't the best way to get a tip, right?"

"Ignore her," Paige said as she stepped up beside Anna and handed over the money to Marty while holding two cold sodas from the fridge in the other. "Keep the change."

"Thanks." He headed back toward his car parked in the driveway, engine still running. "See you all at the trail ride."

Anna stared after him as if he'd just spoken in Icelandic. "What in the world is he talking about?"

"Yum, this smells awesome," Paige said as she turned toward the living room.

Anna followed. "What are you not telling me?"

Paige sighed as she slid the pizza box onto the coffee table that had been sitting in the same spot Anna's entire life.

"I'm going to kill Marty for spilling the beans before I had time to talk to you."

Concern twisted inside Anna's middle. "Explain."

"They're having a charity trail ride at the Peak View Ranch this weekend, and they decided to give the proceeds to you to help pay for your medical bills, a new car, getting back on your feet."

Anna was already shaking her head before Paige finished. "I can't accept that."

"Why not?"

"Because they're my bills, and I'll pay them."

Paige crossed her arms. "How many times have you given to charity by making one of those extra-dollar donations at the grocery? Slipped money into a jar for someone going through chemo? Why is it okay for you to help others but not accept help yourself?"

"Because a lot of people don't have the ability to earn the money to pay for those things. I do."

"You planning on taking a couple of extra jobs to pay for all that, because I know those medical bills alone are going to be huge. It'll take you the rest of your life to pay them off. In case you haven't noticed, no one's getting rich being a librarian."

"I'll do what's necessary. Those trail ride funds could go to a lot more deserving causes."

Paige's expression tightened with irritation. "Why do you see yourself as not deserving?"

"That's not what I said. I just don't want to be seen as not being able to take care of myself, like I can't get by without handouts."

Paige shook her head. "My God, that old woman really did a number on you."

Anna didn't have to ask what Paige was talking about. It wasn't the first time her best friend had expressed her thoughts about how Helena had raised her.

"There's nothing wrong with wanting to be responsible."

"You can't see it, but she made you believe that what you can expect from life is limited and that you can't depend on other people so you shouldn't even try. That's a mighty sorry way of living one's life, if you ask me."

"I didn't ask you." Anna knew the response was too sharp considering Paige had done so much for her. But maybe she'd allowed Paige to do too much already. "I'm sorry. I don't mean to sound ungrateful. I'm very grateful. You're the best friend anyone could ever ask for."

Paige sank onto the couch. "Then why don't you listen to me?"

"I could ask the same question," Anna said as she sat on the opposite end of the couch. "You make changing how I look at the world sound as easy as changing my socks."

"Sure, it's not easy, but it's not as hard as shoving the mountains farther to the west either." Paige sighed. "I just want you to be happy, to have a better life than Helena has had, than your mother had. Just because you're related to them doesn't mean you have to follow in their footsteps."

Paige's words echoed over and over in Anna's mind as the conversation ceased, replaced by mindlessly watching a singing competition on an old TV the thieves hadn't bothered to take and eating pizza that no longer held her interest.

Could she change her way of thinking? Had she already started despite a little voice in her head trying to convince her it was too risky? Maybe managing one's expectations and being self-reliant to a fault seemed like abdicating happiness to Paige, but it was safe. And Anna couldn't quite kick the idea that feeling safe was exactly what she needed right now.

DESPITE TELLING PAIGE to go home and sleep in her own bed, her friend refused. She didn't leave until it was time to go to work at the library the next morning, and she only did that after she elicited a promise from Anna that she would promptly respond to all check-up texts Paige planned to send throughout the day.

When Paige finally pulled out of the driveway, Anna breathed a sigh of relief. For the first time in weeks, she was well and truly alone. But even though it's what she'd been longing for, a momentary wave of concern washed over her. What if something happened in between Paige's texts?

She shook her head to try to dislodge the worries and headed to the kitchen to eat some of the French toast Paige had made while Anna was in the shower. When she took the first bite, she closed her eyes and savored the syrupy flavor. Once she'd enjoyed her solitary breakfast and washed the dishes, she considered what to do with her day. What she needed to do was get back to work because she'd blown through all of her paid leave for the year, but Paige had said if she tried to come back too soon she would have the town officials change the locks on the library's doors.

But after taking a few minutes to go through the pile of bills already residing on her kitchen counter, she had to do something to start whittling away at what she owed. An unexpected memory floated to the front of her thoughts, a long-ago dream that had not come to fruition just as her grandmother's teaching would have predicted.

She retreated to the corner of her bedroom that held her desk. The laptop that had sat atop it was gone who knew where, but what she sought should be in one of the drawers. She flipped to the back of her neatly organized file folders until she found the one holding her brief flirtation with trying to become a published author.

She remembered the sting of the rejection letters inside from three different publishing companies, all of which had arrived on the same day. It had seemed like overwhelming evidence that her grandmother had been right, that she should be satisfied to have a regular job, a regular home in a regular town. After all, lots of people would be happy to have the comfortable life Anna had. She could hear Helena's words as clear as if her grandmother was standing next to her, speaking them anew as if Anna had forgotten the countless previous utterances of the same.

She remembered how she'd originally thrown the rejection letters in the trash, but something had later made her pull them out and file them away. She honestly couldn't say what had caused her to change her mind because she'd been convinced that writing books wasn't in her future. She'd thought that reading mystery series, even putting reviews in the library's newsletter, was as far as her love affair with the genre would go.

But what if she tried again? She'd read a lot more series since then, internalized what made a good mystery novel, an interesting protagonist. And she had access to writing resources through her job. It couldn't hurt to try, especially if she went into it with the idea that if nothing else it might be fun to create her own stories instead of only reading those formed in the minds of others.

However, even if she was able to write something publishable, it would take a long time before it ever saw the light of day. She needed more immediate income. Maybe she, like Paige, should get a second job.

She mulled the possibilities as she wandered around her house. Despite the fact that she'd wanted some privacy, by halfway through the day she was feeling cooped up. Telling herself that exercise was good for recovery, she grabbed her wallet and keys and headed out. It was a gorgeous day, one of those Montana days when the sky was so incredibly blue it almost didn't seem real.

Deciding not to test Paige's promise to change the locks on the library if she saw her there, she instead headed toward the cluster of downtown businesses in search of some lunch. Luckily, her house wasn't a long walk from the small business district that made up Logan Springs because by the time she reached the Big Sky Café, she was feeling kind of wiped out. It appeared her recovery had not quite caught up to her desire to be completely back to normal.

But she didn't want anyone to see that, so she took a deep breath and held herself up straighter before she pulled open the door to the restaurant and stepped inside.

"Hey, didn't expect to see you out and about this soon," Lena said as she picked up some dirty dishes at a table close to the door. "Having lunch with Paige?"

Anna shook her head. "Just me."

Lena's eyes widened a little. "Did you walk here?"

Anna managed a smile. "Yeah, good exercise."

"Well, right now I think you need to sit before you fall down." Lena nodded at the table she'd just cleared. "I'll be back to wipe it off."

Anna took the proffered table, thankful the restaurant wasn't super busy. The main lunch rush was over, and several of the people sitting at other tables didn't look familiar. She didn't know every resident of Logan Springs, but if she had to guess she'd say at least some of her fellow diners were tourists headed to Yellowstone.

A day in the park actually sounded really nice, but it would be a while before she could indulge in that outing. Not only did she not have enough energy yet, but when she did she needed to spend her time working and earning her way out of debt. Not to mention she no longer had a car in which to drive to the park.

Lena was back a few moments later with a menu and a

wet cloth to wash away the mess from the previous customers. "I could have arranged a delivery for you."

"I needed to get outside and feel the sun on my face. The time in the hospital and in rehab made me think I might never feel it again."

"I hear you. I had to spend one night in the hospital when I was in high school, and I thought I was going to go crazy. Who is supposed to feel better constantly being poked and having to listen to beeping machines all the time?"

"An excellent question."

"So do you know what you want, or do you need a minute to look at the menu?"

"Do you have the chicken noodle soup today? I think I could eat a bowl of that as big as my head."

"We do, indeed. One head-size bowl of soup coming right up."

As she waited for her meal, Anna spoke to a few people she did recognize—the mayor, a couple of ladies who were regular library patrons, and Marty.

"Are you stalking me?" Anna teased when she saw him.

"Really small town."

She chuckled as he picked up his takeout order and hurried back out the door.

When Lena returned with the soup, she slipped into the chair across from Anna. "So, did sleeping in your own bed feel like a million bucks last night?"

"Definitely better than that thing at the hospital they called a bed." She ate a spoonful of the hot soup. "Delicious as always."

"Thanks. All-purpose, make-you-feel-better soup."

Anna thought of the conversation she'd had with Paige the night before, about how a benefit trail ride had been planned without her knowledge.

"Can I talk to you about something?"

"Sure."

"Paige told me that your family plans to give the proceeds of a trail ride this weekend to me, but that's not necessary. There are so many other ways that money could be put to good use."

"What could be better than helping one of our own?"

"I'm sure there are others who need it more than I do, like the people Roman helps out at the free clinic. I'll be fine."

"The word has already been put out, and literally everyone thinks it's a good idea. You are universally liked, and you've had a bigger string of bad luck than any one person deserves."

"I just…" Anna searched for a reason that would not make her sound like some sort of anti-charity zealot.

"Listen, if it's the whole accepting charity thing, then accept the help now when you really need it and pay it forward when you can."

While a large part of her still hated the idea of accepting money that had come out of the pockets of her neighbors, she swallowed any further objections. She would pay it forward. She didn't know how yet, but she would.

CHAPTER NINE

ROMAN DROVE SOUTH out of Livingston, wishing that he'd stayed at the ranch last night instead of at home. But he'd had a long day at the office followed by seeing a lot of patients at the free clinic. It seemed there were more patients every week, people who were barely getting by or falling through the cracks. He felt guilty sometimes, to be so fortunate when so many had so little. If his family hosted any future charity trail rides, he was going to suggest the proceeds go to the clinic—not for his own benefit because he donated his time, but for the supplies and expenses necessary to operate.

But today's trail ride was all about Anna. His pulse jumped at the idea of seeing her again, spending the day with her. First up was chauffeuring her to the ranch since Paige was working.

It had been a week since he'd delivered Anna to her welcome-home party, and he'd lost count of the number of times he'd thought about her. Each time he did rounds at the hospital and saw someone else in the bed she'd occupied. When he passed the drive-in where he'd purchased her celebratory milkshake. And during unexpected moments that had nothing to do with her.

It was a strange sensation to suddenly think so much about a person you'd known for years, with whom you'd shared the hallways of the small Logan Springs High School, a person who'd never elicited feelings of attraction before. Even stranger that the attraction had started when she'd been bruised, cut, weak and wearing a hospital gown. But it wasn't just her physical appearance that caused the attraction, though when he had taken the time to really look at her he'd been surprised he'd somehow missed the soft, simple beauty there. Despite her frustrations with her recovery, there was no denying she was a kind soul, someone who cared for others. He could think of nothing more attractive.

When Paige had called him to see if he could pick up Anna this morning, he'd had difficulty hiding how much he liked the idea.

The balloons were gone from her street when he drove down it. She was already sitting on the front porch, and he took that as a good sign that she was looking forward to the day. He couldn't deny he hoped she'd also been looking forward to seeing him.

But as she approached his truck, he saw the concern on her face. She must have realized it because she exchanged it for a smile. Not one that said, "I'm thrilled to see you," but a smile nonetheless.

"Hey, looks like you're recovering well," he said as she climbed into the truck.

"Stronger every day. I'm headed back to work on Monday."

"That's good. Just don't overdo it until you get used to working again."

He backed out of her driveway and as he drove through town and toward the ranch, she stared out her window.

"You okay?" He wondered if her mood had anything to do with the conversation she'd had with Lena. Was she preparing herself to be embarrassed by the attention? Or was it as Lena had suggested, that Anna was really averse to accepting charity?

She nodded without looking at him, at least for a few seconds. But then she surprised him by glancing his way and saying, "I feel really weird about accepting people's hard-earned money. It feels like mooching."

"Did you ask anyone for money?"

"No."

"Did you expect it?"

"No, of course not."

"Then it's not mooching. It's neighbors helping neighbors. That's just how we do things around here. You should know that. You've been on the giving end."

"You talked to Lena, didn't you?"

"Yes, but she was right."

"It just feels wrong."

"Why?"

She sighed and clasped her hands tightly in her lap. "I was always taught that you take care of your own responsibilities, that you never depend on others to solve your problems for you."

He had no doubt that's exactly what Helena Kenner had taught her granddaughter, and it was hard to escape the teachings embedded early by those who raised you. He'd seen it in the occasional patient who didn't believe in vaccines or antibiotics because that's what they'd been taught from a young age.

What was the best way to set her mind at ease?

"Let me ask you this. Would you feel the same way if Paige had been the one in the accident? Would you think less of her for accepting help?"

He glanced over in time to see the light-bulb expression on her face.

"Why did you have to make a good point?"

He laughed as he made the turn into the ranch behind another truck pulling a horse trailer.

"Besides," he said, "this will be fun. I haven't been out for a ride purely for pleasure in a long time."

"How often do you get to see your family?"

"As often as I can. It's hard to carve out large chunks of time, especially on the days I work at the free clinic." While driving the rest of the way to the house, he told her about the clinic and the important part it played in the health care of the area. Judging by the questions she asked about it, she seemed genuinely interested.

"Maybe if my luck changes and I win the lottery, I'll pay this forward," she said, indicating all the people and horses gathering near the barns, "to your clinic."

"I like the sound of that plan."

After he parked, he accompanied her toward the crowd. They ended up stopping several times as people wished her well and Anna thanked them for their generosity.

As they stepped away from Freddie Stephenson, the mayor of Logan Springs, he noticed Lena waving at them from her post next to Dinah behind the refreshment table that offered coffee and fresh doughnuts from Dinah's bakery.

Roman snagged a bear claw and a coffee.

"Someone needs his caffeine and sugar this morning," Dinah said.

"I've been dreaming about this bear claw since last night. I might marry this bear claw."

Beside him, Anna laughed a little. "Well, I have to try one if they're good enough to inspire marriage proposals."

Dinah and Lena's brothers, Brandon and Matt, approached with Wes.

"Wow, when was the last time all the McQueen cousins got the same day off?" Roman's brother asked.

"The benefit of being the boss," Brandon said, referencing his river outfitting business. "If my employees can't run things without me for one day, I haven't done a very good job of hiring."

"Amen," said Dinah and Lena, almost in unison, and took turns giving Brandon a high five.

"Just got lucky." Matt, a ranger in Yellowstone, didn't have the luxury of making his own schedule.

"Thank you all so much for doing this," Anna said, her

cheeks flushed with embarrassment. "I don't know how to thank you."

Just then, his dad called out that the ride would commence in fifteen minutes.

"Is there anything I can do here to help while you all are gone?" Anna asked.

Everyone paused in their movements and stared at her, then at Roman. Wes was the first one to speak.

"We've got a really calm horse for you to ride so you can go, too."

"Oh, no, I couldn't do that even if I hadn't recently had my brain knocked around in my head. I've never been on a horse."

"You can ride with me," Roman said, drawing all the attention toward him. And, damn it, he saw more than one barely suppressed grin.

"I'm sure you'll have a better time on your own," Anna said, the color in her cheeks deepening.

Was it just an extension of her earlier embarrassment, or was this specifically caused by the idea of riding so close to him? He found he really wanted to find out.

"You'll be perfectly safe."

"And how better to get your first ride under your belt than to go with someone as experienced as Roman?" Lena did a better job of hiding her ulterior motive, but he could still see the mischief in her eyes.

So what if they could tell he liked Anna? He just needed them not to make a big, obvious deal out of it because he had no idea what he was going to do about his attraction and how Anna might react. He got the feeling it was a tread lightly type of situation.

"I don't know," Anna said.

"At least come meet the horse," Roman said, needing to get her away from his family for a few minutes. "Then you can decide."

She nodded and he escorted her to the barn where his horse, Juniper, was in her stall. Before he opened the stall door, he wanted to allow Anna a chance to meet and hopefully be a bit more comfortable with the mare.

"This is Juniper. I've had her since the summer after I completed undergrad."

Anna tentatively held up her hand to Juniper's nose, and the mare sniffed at her. When Anna giggled at the contact, he smiled.

"It tickles," she said.

"She likes you." He moved closer to Anna without even thinking about it. "I promise I won't let you fall."

Because he realized that was probably her chief worry, not some imagined nervousness about being close to him.

She ventured her hand up so that she could rub between Juniper's eyes, and the horse liked the attention. "Okay."

Because Anna hadn't sounded sure of her answer, he showed her every step of getting Juniper ready to ride. If the others left without them, that was fine. They could catch up. It was more important for Anna to be comfortable. He wondered how successful he'd been quelling her fear when he pulled her up in front of him and felt her shaking.

Hoping it would help, he placed one of his hands atop where she held the saddle horn. "Ready?"

After a moment, she nodded and he eased Juniper out of the barn. Outside, he saw the rest of the riders stretched out along the inside of the fence line. They would ride that for a while, until they hit the spot where the river turned. Then they'd parallel the river before turning toward the foothills.

It took a few minutes, but Anna seemed to gradually relax. By the time they reached the river, it no longer felt as if her spine was an iron pole.

"It's so beautiful out here," she said, sounding as if she hadn't lived her entire life in the same valley. "I don't take enough time to really enjoy it instead of taking it for granted. A near-death experience makes you realize things like that."

"You're welcome to come here anytime and ride. If I'm not here, I'm sure Dad or one of my brothers would be happy to give you lessons so you could feel comfortable riding on your own."

"That's a kind offer, but this is about as far as I think my comfort level is going to extend. Besides, I'll be working a lot."

"Are you sure you're ready to go back to work?"

"If I don't, I might go stir crazy. I've managed to fill my time this week cleaning, looking for cars online, writing, but I need a sense of normality again so I can stop thinking about what happened and worrying that my brain might decide to do a Rip Van Winkle again."

She'd already been assured that was unlikely, but then he knew from personal experience the power of one's mind to worry that a past illness might return—rational or not.

He maneuvered Juniper along the trail, taking a moment to drink in the beauty of their surroundings. Even though he'd grown up on this land, Mother Nature never ceased to amaze him. Even though he'd enjoyed the years he'd spent in Washington for his education, had appreciated the natural beauty there, coming back here had never been a question. And when his mom died, he was even more glad he'd made the decision to open his practice nearby.

He sucked in a breath that felt like someone had stabbed him in the chest. It must have been audible because Anna looked over her shoulder at him.

"Is something wrong?" The worry in her voice made guilt well up inside him.

"No. Was just thinking about how Mom used to come riding out here. I remember this one time after I'd been home from a hospitalization for a while, she bundled me up and took me on a ride. There was a fall chill in the air, and I remember leaning back against her and feeling her warmth, feeling as if she could protect me from a grizzly bear if one showed up."

"She was a wonderful woman."

"Yeah, she was."

"You were very lucky. I can't imagine what it must have been like growing up here, with a big family."

"I've always been thankful, especially when I was sick,

but I don't think I really grasped how good I had it with my family until I started working as a doctor."

"You see a lot of brokenness?"

"Yeah. It's hard to see because it's something I can't fix. Not with any amount of medicine."

"Is that why you started working at the free clinic?"

"Partly, maybe."

"But there's another reason?"

He looked up at the wide expanse of blue sky and the smattering of fluffy white clouds. "It had more to do with needing something else, anything, to fill my time so I wouldn't think about how my mom had been there for me and how there was nothing I could do to save her."

Anna turned so she could look at him. "That wasn't your fault."

"I know that. Didn't make it hurt any less."

"I wish I knew what to say to make it not hurt anymore."

Something moved in the area of his heart at the kindness in her words, and for a crazy moment he wanted very much to kiss her. But if there was ever a first kiss between them, it wasn't going to be with half the valley watching.

"Thank you."

He wasn't sure if it was because she felt safer and steadier facing forward or she picked up on some of his thoughts, but she turned back around. They followed the other riders as they pointed their horses toward the Gallatin Range.

"How you liking it?" Wes called back to Anna a few minutes later.

"It's fun."

Once Wes had returned his attention to his date, Roman asked, "Are you really having fun or just putting on a brave face?"

"Really. I wouldn't have done this on my own, but I'm glad I'm here now."

So was he.

★

WHEN THE FLATNESS of the valley began to turn upward into rolling hills that eventually led to the impressive peaks in the distance, the riders ahead of them started reining in their horses and sliding out of their saddles.

"Lunchtime," Roman said behind her, his voice a deep rumble she could feel in her back.

"Oh, I didn't bring anything."

"Lucky for you, I came prepared." He halted Juniper and got to the ground. Then he placed a hand at her waist, causing the most delicious shiver to pass through her body. "Swing your leg over."

She did as he directed, and in the next moment he had his hands on both sides of her waist, helping her to the ground as if she weighed nothing. Though it was slight by any rational person's standards, the amount of contact between their bodies was more than her poor, battered brain could handle, so she stepped away as soon as her feet were on the ground. Unfortunately, she wasn't as steady as she should be and stumbled on rubbery legs. Roman reached out to keep her from falling, just as he'd promised he would.

"Thanks."

"Here, hang on for a moment while I get our lunch," he said as he patted the edge of the saddle.

She gripped the saddle as indicated, hoping Juniper didn't decide to dance sideways.

Roman retrieved what looked like soft, insulated packs from a saddlebag, then he extended his arm.

"I'm good, thanks. Sort of like getting off a boat back onto dry land." Or at least how she imagined it would be since she'd never been on an ocean-going vessel. She'd only seen the ocean once, when she'd gone to a librarians' convention in Seattle.

Roman didn't question her assertion, but she noticed that he adjusted his pace to hers as they headed for a pretty spot next to a creek that ran out of the mountains and emptied into the Yellowstone River.

"I didn't think to bring a blanket to sit on," he said.

"No need. A little grass isn't going to hurt anything."

To prove to him and, honestly, herself that she was just wobbly from being in the saddle and nothing more, she willed herself to not topple as she sat on the ground. Once safely down, she took a deep, fortifying breath and listened to the burble of the little creek. All around them, the other riders were finding their own spots to sit and have lunch. Beside her, Roman sank to the ground and pulled two thick sandwiches and bottles of water from the insulated packs.

"Hope you like turkey and ham," he said.

"Sounds great."

For a couple of minutes, they ate in silence. She let the sounds of various conversations, the soft trickle of the creek, and the pleasant breeze soothe away the buzzy nervousness she'd felt since she'd seen Roman pull up in her driveway. Even though she knew that Paige was indeed working, she had no doubt that her best friend calling Roman to be her taxi driver over to the ranch was still calculated. She'd gotten it into her head that Anna and Roman were perfect for each other. Maybe that was true in Anna's fantasies, but reality was often a different story. Even if he was attracted to her, she had a hard time believing it would last. Opposites attracting was way more believable in fiction.

But were they really opposites?

They had more things in common than she would have ever imagined, but that little voice in her head still whispered that their lives were just too different for anything other than friendship to ever work. But having him as a friend would be nice. Eventually, she'd get past her infatuation.

Her peaceful moments ended when other riders started coming over to ask how she was doing, expressing gratitude that she was on the mend, and asking if she knew what had caused her accident. She didn't know how many times she responded with "Fine," "Thank you," and "No, it's a blank." By the time the parade of well-wishers faded, it was time to start the ride back and she'd only eaten about a quarter of her sandwich.

When she started to stand, Roman rested a hand on her forearm.

"Go ahead and eat. It's not a race back to the barn."

"But they're doing this for me. I should be there."

"You are under no obligations here, Anna. Stay, enjoy your lunch. We can catch up with them in a few minutes."

As she scanned the crowd, he seemed to be right. No one was looking at her with a gaze that asked why she wasn't preparing to leave like the rest of them. When anyone met her gaze, they just smiled and went back to mounting up. She honestly didn't know what to do. Part of her wanted to experience the quiet of this spot once everyone had ridden away, to sit only with Roman and maybe talk some more as they had on the way out. But that same situation made a flock of frantic butterflies start beating their wings in her stomach, too.

"Sorry if this is too overwhelming," he said, pointing toward the retreating horses and riders.

"It's fine. I know everyone means well."

"I'm around people so much that I didn't think how taxing this might be for you even without the physical fatigue."

"I interact with people at the library all the time."

He looked over and smiled. "I doubt that's the same."

He was right about that. Even though a number of people liked to chat, most of the social interaction happened with Paige or the volunteers. Now that she thought about it, most of her contact with the public had to do with library-related topics. Even in her job, she wasn't fully engaged with those around her. She really needed to change that.

"I hope I don't come across as rude."

"Not at all. Maybe a little shy, but seems you have a pretty good job for someone more introverted."

Is that how he saw her, like a turtle happier inside her shell? Is that how everyone saw her? She realized they were right. After all, the shell offered protection from things that could hurt you, and she'd been convinced she had to protect herself from being hurt any further.

It hit her hard that while she'd been busy recommending books that hopefully were leading people to dream of and work toward better lives, she hadn't been living her own advice.

"Can I ask you something personal?" Roman asked.

"Um, sure." She could always decline to answer.

"When we were talking about my mom, it made me wonder about yours. I think I remember seeing her once, but I'm not sure that's an accurate memory."

She stared out across the creek at the cattle grazing nearby. Her mother wasn't one of her favorite topics, but then she remembered how Roman had opened up to her about his own mother.

"It's possible, though she wasn't here often." Only when she'd wanted something, usually money. No matter how many times Helena had told her no, she wasn't getting one red cent, she would still try when she hit rock bottom. "But she died when I was fourteen."

"I'm sorry."

Anna shrugged then wondered how many times she'd had the same reaction when someone found out about her mother being gone and expressed sympathy.

"Truth is I didn't really know her very well. When I was little, it hurt to think she never wanted me. But I guess I just grew used to it."

"I wish she'd been a better mother to you. When I think about how good I had it with my mom, I feel guilty sometimes."

"You should never feel guilty, just grateful."

"No doubt there."

She took another bite of her sandwich, honestly surprised she still had an appetite in the wake of talking about her mother.

"If I haven't been too nosy already, do you mind me asking about your dad?"

She glanced over at Roman and was struck again by just how handsome he was, especially with that aura of kindness and compassion that was as much a part of him as his long legs and kissable lips. That thought caused her to shift her gaze away, probably so quickly it looked suspicious.

"I don't know who he is. Mom never said. And if Helena ever knew, she didn't tell me. All I know is what I overheard one night when they were fighting in the kitchen during one of Mom's rare visits. He evidently had been Mom's boss somewhere she'd worked, and when he found out she was pregnant he didn't want to have anything to do with her or me. I suspect he was already married."

She didn't know why she told him that last bit, but it felt like a relief to say it out loud. It made her realize just how few people she'd had to confide in during her life. But she hadn't even told Paige about her suspicions about her father. So why was she telling Roman?

Because despite your nervousness around him, he's easy to talk to. And you've held stuff in for so long, you didn't even realize it's been festering for years.

"That must have been hard to come to terms with," he said, thankfully not resorting to the "I'm sorry" most people would have offered in his situation.

"Honestly, it just seemed par for the course. Sure, when I was little, I used to dream about what it would be like to have a mom and dad at home like my classmates, but I never really knew what it was like. My existence was always just grandmother-as-parent. Even though I had parents out there somewhere, I didn't know my father and my mother was never a big part of my life. When she died, I think I was more upset about losing what could have been than what was."

Roman didn't say anything. Maybe he had no idea what words would be appropriate after what she'd revealed. He did, however, reach over and squeeze her hand in silent support. She directed a quick smile in his direction, and despite the nervousness racing through her she didn't move her hand.

After a few moments filled only with the sounds of nature around them, Roman spoke.

"Have you ever thought about trying to find out who your dad is?"

"I flirted with the idea when I was younger, but then I came to the conclusion that if he had no interest in me then he wasn't worth finding."

Part of her expected him to disagree with her, for the healer in him to want to fix the situation so that it had a happy ending. That just wasn't how the world worked sometimes. But he surprised her by nodding as if he understood and maybe even agreed.

"Sometimes it's better if certain people aren't in our lives," he said. "Justin's ex-girlfriend, for example. All she was interested in was what our family has spent decades building. But he figured that out, and now he's going to marry someone who would still love him if he was living in a cardboard box."

"Melody has been through her own trials," she said. "I'm happy for them both."

Anna had felt betrayed by her parents on more than one occasion, but she couldn't imagine what it had been like for Melody. Not only had she lost her family but also her family's legacy, everything she'd ever owned, and for a while her very identity. And scariest of all, she'd almost lost her life. But thankfully all that was behind her now, and it was as if she was a different woman even after being able to reclaim her true identity. Anna wondered if she'd ever seen anyone look happier. What did that kind of happiness feel like? Could she create it for herself?

She couldn't help but look over at Roman and allow herself to dream for a moment before she shifted her gaze to the horses in the distance.

"We should get going. Maybe there are some of those bear claws left."

Roman laughed. "You really didn't like hospital food, did you?"

"Is that a real question?"

His smile widened as he stood without releasing her hand. When he used the connection to help her get to her feet, she got a glimpse of what it might feel like to be with him as more than a friend. In the next moment, she realized how close she was standing to him, facing each other, feeling the very male heat of him, and her heart stuttered before accelerating.

What was even scarier than her own reaction was the look of interest she saw in the eyes staring back at her.

CHAPTER TEN

H E'D SCARED HER without meaning to. Roman had
seen it in her eyes as she looked up at him. But instead
of apologizing, he decided to pretend he hadn't allowed her
to see his attraction and how it had been growing throughout the day. He did his best not to touch her too much as
they made their way toward the back of the line of riders.
But after how much they'd shared until that moment of
intense eye contact, the silence between them now was
making him antsy.

"Did I tell you I went back to the beginning of the Anna
Pigeon series and started reading book one?" he asked.

"No. Are you enjoying it?"

He sighed inwardly. Their words were so stilted and reserved now. "Yeah. I don't typically read fiction much, but
I'm hooked now. Not that I have a lot of time to read."

Their conversation sputtered out again, like a motor dy-
ing. At least they were catching up with the others. He
noticed Wes and his cousins looking back at them, smiling,
then talking among themselves. That didn't bode well.

When they reached the main part of the ranch, some
people were already loading up their horses.

"Thought we lost you guys back there," Lena said then shot Dinah a conspiratorial smile.

"We just took our time eating lunch," he said as he dismounted. "No need to hurry on a trail ride."

"Or when you're having fun," Dinah added.

"Is there a restroom I can use?" Anna asked.

"Sure." He reached up to help her down from the saddle, and for a moment he thought she might refuse to accept it. But her fear of falling must have won out over whatever feelings were stirred up between them. When he had her safely on the ground, he pointed toward the house. "Straight through to the hallway, and it's on your right."

Though he was aware of his cousins watching him, he couldn't take his gaze away from Anna as she made her way toward the house, pausing a few times to exchange a few words with other riders.

"You like her, don't you?" Lena had always been the most observant of all the McQueen cousins. Nothing escaped her attention. It made her a great business owner but an occasionally annoying cousin.

"We're just friends."

"That doesn't answer my question."

After he saw Anna slip through the front door of his family home, he shifted his attention to Lena. "I don't know what I feel, but she's not interested so it doesn't matter."

"What makes you say that?"

"Because I scare her."

"That's ridiculous. You're the least scary person I know."

"Unless you have a needle," Dinah said.

Lena made a shushing hand gesture toward Dinah while still looking at him. "Seriously, what makes you think she's scared of you?"

He shouldn't have said anything, but now he'd already opened his mouth. There was no retracting his words. So he told them about what had happened next to the creek.

"Maybe it's just because she's shy," Lena said.

"I don't think she's dated much." Dinah glanced toward the house, probably making sure Anna wasn't in earshot. "I actually can't remember ever seeing her with anyone. Maybe she's intimidated."

"Why would she be intimidated?"

Lena and Dinah glanced at each other before Lena responded.

"Are you serious? You're a handsome guy, successful, really smart."

He stared at his cousin, trying to figure out her point. "How could those things be intimidating if Anna can lay claim to the same qualities?"

Lena tilted her head slightly to the side. "Maybe because at least part of her doesn't think she does."

"She said that?"

"No. Deduction on my part."

Was Lena right? Could Anna really not know how amazing she was? Who was he kidding? He was only now realizing it, and he'd known her for most of his life. Sure, not well, but enough that he should have been able to at least see hints of the truth.

He was still questioning the entire situation and what he should or shouldn't do about it when he saw Anna come back out of the house. He started toward her without even realizing his brain had made that decision. He got waylaid by a few friends and neighbors the same as she had, and he had to wait while Sheriff Franklin drove past pulling his trailer. By the time he reached where he'd seen Anna, he'd lost sight of her.

As he turned in a circle, he finally spotted her over next to his dad's truck at the end of the house.

"Hey," he said as he approached her. "Are—"

He halted when he saw the look on her face. He'd heard the expression "You look like you've seen a ghost" probably dozens of times in his life, but this was the first time it seemed appropriate. He reached out and grabbed her shoulders, afraid she was about to pass out.

"What's wrong?"

She swallowed visibly. "I remembered something about the wreck."

"That's good." As soon as he said that, he wasn't sure. After all, it appeared that every bit of blood had drained from her face. "What did you remember?"

"I was run off the road by a truck." She pointed in front of her. "One that looked like that."

It was Roman's turn to feel as if he was about to pass out. No, it couldn't be. His dad had gone through a bad patch after his wife died. He'd tried to drown his sorrows, had even run off the road while intoxicated. Thankfully, he hadn't hurt himself or anyone else, and partially thanks to Melody giving him a good talking-to, he'd given up that destructive way of dealing with his grief.

Hadn't he?

Roman scanned the area for his dad but didn't see him. He'd deal with him later. Now he had to focus on Anna.

"Here, let's sit on the porch for a minute."

He thought she might refuse, but then she allowed him to steer her up the couple of steps and toward two rocking chairs.

"Would you like something to drink?"

"No, I'm fine." She lifted her hand from the arm of the chair, as if she might be reaching to stop him, before lowering it again.

He recognized the look on her face now: that of someone who'd just experienced a panic attack and didn't want to be left alone. He reached over and took her hand in his, and she let him. That was evidence enough that the memory had really shaken her.

"I think he hit me."

Unable to help himself, he looked at the passenger side of his dad's truck. There was no damage visible, but she could be misremembering actually making contact with the other vehicle.

"Take your time, but tell me everything you remember."

She closed her eyes as people tended to do when trying to recover elusive memories. "I was coming back from Bozeman. I'd been to a workshop for librarians at the university." She paused, and her forehead scrunched as if she was literally trying to squeeze a memory out of her brain like water from a sponge. After a few seconds, she shook her head. "Then there's a big blank between when I left to come home and when the accident happened."

"It's okay. This is a good sign. Don't push it. If more memories come back, they'll likely do so when you least expect it like this one did today."

"It's so frustrating having this big empty space where it's almost as if I didn't even exist."

He squeezed her hand. "You did."

She offered a shaky smile, and it was amazing how even that little bit of brightness affected him. In that moment he wanted to pull her into his arms, to protect her from anything in the world that might dare think about hurting her. But that could very well scare her as much as the accident had. While no doubt strong and determined, there was also a skittish kitten quality about Anna that caused his protective instincts to come roaring to the fore.

Anna glanced over at his dad's truck, and his insides knotted. He needed to find out where his dad was that day without his dad knowing. Because if this was all just a coincidence and his dad had been nowhere near the interstate that day, he didn't want to remind him of that dark period when his dad had not only struggled with how to process his grief but also with who he even was without the love of his life.

"The tires were bigger," Anna said, cutting into his thoughts.

"What?"

"The tires on the truck that hit me, they were different. Those huge ones that make a lot of noise. The truck was so tall I couldn't even see the driver."

Roman breathed a sigh of relief. It hadn't been his dad. And part of him felt guilty for having thought his dad had relapsed and lied to them all about it.

"You need to report this," he said.

"It probably won't do any good. I mean, it's not like there are cameras all along the interstate. And evidently no one else was around because no witnesses have come forward."

"You never know, and it couldn't hurt." He spotted Parker talking to Wes and whistled to get their attention. When they looked toward the house, he waved them over.

"What's up?" Wes asked as he and his best friend stepped up to the edge of the porch.

Roman didn't miss how Wes noticed his hand wrapped around Anna's and lifted a brow in question. Roman ignored him and got to the point.

"Anna remembered some details from her accident." He shifted his gaze to Anna, who looked really tired. After this, he was taking her home and making her rest. "Tell Parker what you told me. Every little detail might help."

She didn't look convinced, but she repeated everything she'd told him, even adding that she thought she'd seen brake lights before her car went over the embankment.

Had the driver started to stop and then driven away instead, not wanting to be responsible for what he'd just caused? An unusual and unexpected rage rose up inside Roman, but he clamped down on it so Anna wouldn't see. But he wasn't so lucky with his brother. Wes had a lot of questions in his eyes, but he didn't give them voice. Roman didn't think he'd be so lucky when Anna wasn't around.

But why should he mind if Wes brought it up in conversation? Everyone who heard what Anna just said ought to be angry on her behalf. It was bad enough to run someone off the road, but to then pause only long enough to make the conscious decision to leave them to their fate to save one's own ass—that was what made Roman want to smash something. And totally against his nature, he envisioned that being the face of the person who left Anna alone to die. Thank God that couple had found her.

"If you think of anything else, let me know," Parker said as he handed a business card to Anna.

"You think what little bit I can remember will help at all?"

"It might be a long shot, but you never know. I've seen stranger things happen."

When Wes and Parker walked away, Roman noticed that the rest of the people who'd come out for the trail ride had vacated the premises. And Anna looked as if she might fall over any minute.

"Let's get you home."

"I hate for you to have to go out of your way again."

He smiled as he stood, not letting go of her hand as he helped her to her feet. "It's not like you live in Missoula."

Either she was so tired she somehow wasn't processing he still held her hand as they headed toward his truck or she was worried she might topple over without his support. He only let go when she was safely seated and buckled into the passenger seat. When he was seated in his own and backing out of his parking spot, he glanced over to see her leaning back against the headrest, her eyes closed.

"I'm sorry if we overdid it today. I may have overestimated how much you were ready to do."

She looked toward him but without lifting her head. "It's not that. I had a nice time, really. It's so beautiful out here."

He wasn't buying that she hadn't overtaxed herself, but he wouldn't argue and tire her even more.

"I promise," she said, as if she'd read his mind. "It's that I'm having a hard time imagining someone just leaving me like that. I could never do that, drive away when someone might be hurt or worse."

"Of course, you couldn't. You're a good person, Anna. I have never heard one bad word about you."

"I doubt that. Nobody is liked by everyone."

"No, really. People care about you because you care about them. Maybe you're not obvious or flashy about it, but that's what makes it even more genuine."

She looked at him as if he was speaking a language she couldn't comprehend. "I don't know what to say."

"You don't have to say anything."

And she didn't, not for the rest of the drive back to her house. Not as he escorted her inside and grabbed a bottle of water from her fridge and gave it to her.

"Thanks for the ride home," she said as she took it. "For everything. I'm sorry for the times I've been cranky."

He ignored the hint that while genuine, her words were also a dismissal. "Everyone is cranky when they don't feel good. Trust me, I know."

She smiled a little. "Yeah, I suppose you don't have a parade of happy people traipsing through your office."

"Not usually. No 'I feel great. I think I'll go see the doctor today.'"

She smiled again then took a drink of her water. He sank into the chair adjacent to the couch.

"You don't have to stay. I'm fine."

"I don't have anywhere I need to be." And if he went back to the ranch, he had no doubt Wes was going to grill him about that whole hand-holding thing. And Roman didn't really know how to answer.

Well, that was a lie, wasn't it? He liked Anna, liked her more every time he was around her. Holding her hand had felt peaceful and exciting at the same time. But he didn't know what to do about it, or how he would respond if questioned by Wes or any other member of his family. Whatever was happening, it felt private.

"Really, I'm probably just going to take a shower and then a nap."

"Feel free."

Her eyebrows lifted in surprise.

He smiled. "I promise to be a perfect gentleman and stay out here where I belong."

"No, I didn't mean—"

"I know. And I know you're a strong woman, independent. I'm not saying you're not. But I'd like to stay for a while—not as a doctor, but as a friend."

Perhaps a friend who was having thoughts of being more, but she didn't need to hear that right now. She needed to rest, not worry about the guy sitting in her living room.

"I don't think I'm the only one with a stubborn streak," she said.

The hint of humor in her voice made his smile widen. "No, ma'am, you are not."

She stared at him as if considering her options, but the day's activity had tapped out her energy reserves. He knew the signs. He could remember feeling them when he'd been recovering from his own health issues. Evidently acknowledging that this wasn't a fight she'd win, she pushed herself to her feet.

"Feel free to watch TV or read anything you can find on the shelf," she said as she pointed toward a stuffed bookshelf at the end of the room.

He watched her as she disappeared down the hallway and had a thought that would likely get him kicked out of her house for good. He imagined holding that soft, small hand of hers and following her to the bedroom.

Feeling that he was somehow betraying her trust, he shook his head and stalked to the bookshelf. Not surprisingly, it was stuffed with mystery novels along with an eclectic selection of nonfiction titles. He spotted the same book he was currently reading at home when he could snatch a few minutes here and there. As he pulled it from the shelf, he heard the shower turn on. Despite trying to keep his thoughts elsewhere, he imagined Anna being naked just beyond that bathroom door. He should feel guilty, but he was a man, damn it. A man with eyes. And Anna Kenner was the sort of pretty that caught you unaware but never let you go, either.

Trying to block out the sound of the flowing water and the thought of what it was hitting, he stretched out on Anna's couch and found the spot where he'd stopped reading at home. But when a door opened down the hall a few minutes later, he realized he'd been attempting to read the same page the entirety of the time Anna had been in the bathroom.

He looked up thinking that Anna might reappear. Instead, he heard another door close. And if he wasn't mistaken, the soft click of a lock followed. He hated that she felt so uncomfortable with him in her house, but it was too late to do anything about it now. He wasn't about to leave her alone. If something happened, he'd never forgive himself. She'd be on her own soon enough, but it wasn't going to be today.

WHAT WAS HE doing out there? Despite being exhausted, Anna lay in her bed wide awake alternately staring at the ceiling, her closed door and the clock. After so much time in the hospital and rehab, she'd wanted nothing more than to sleep at normal times like a normal person. And yet here she was in bed before it was even dark outside. She looked at the clock again only to find the time hadn't changed since she'd last looked. When was Paige going to get here?

She rolled onto her side, hugging one of the extra pillows and trying not to wonder what it would be like to lay her head against Roman's chest instead. Judging by how her body had reacted when he'd simply held her hand, she might very well combust.

How many times had she needed to remind herself on the way home that Roman was just being kind, a friend? She couldn't let her feelings get carried away, as they'd threatened to do the moment he'd taken her hand in his. She'd initially thought the head rush was from the sudden recollection of memories from the day of the crash, but now she didn't think so. Sure, the memory of the truck hitting her, or nearly hitting her—she wasn't sure which—had startled her, but that couldn't account for the surge of warmth through her body when Roman had touched her.

How was she supposed to sleep knowing that he was just down the short hallway?

CHAPTER ELEVEN

A ND YET, SLEEP she did.

She came awake slowly, disoriented. Like the cogs in a lazy wheel, she remembered the events of the day. She blinked the sleep from her eyes and looked at the clock. The red display numbers read 9:14 p.m., and with that knowledge came a twisted-up, conflicted feeling in her chest. Roman would be gone by now. She tried convincing herself that was a good thing, but she couldn't quite do it.

It was also inescapably true that she enjoyed spending time with Roman, even if she ran the risk of falling for him. Who was she kidding? She'd started falling for the man the day he'd brought in that silly ladder poster and the promise of a milkshake.

Her stomach growled, reminding her that she hadn't eaten since the sandwich beside the creek with Roman. She closed her eyes and replayed how it had felt to ride in front of him, his arms around her. How when he'd helped her down from the horse, she'd had to fight the desire to wrap her arms around his neck despite all the sets of eyes that would have witnessed it and her shame when he had to tell her he only wanted to be friends. The considerate way he'd allowed her extra time to not only finish eating but also to relax, away from all the well-meaning people on the trail ride.

He would make someone a wonderful husband someday. And she couldn't deny that she could all too easily imagine herself in the role of wife. Was she changing? Only days ago, she wouldn't have even dreamed of such a thing.

She took a deep breath and made her way to the bathroom. When she finished brushing her teeth, she was surprised to find the house still quiet. Had Paige fallen asleep? Or had her friends decided she was okay to be alone after all? Despite her repeatedly telling them exactly that, a flutter of fear caused her to stop halfway up the hall and press her hand to her chest.

Stop being silly. You're fine.

When she reached the living room, it wasn't Paige she found sleeping on her couch. Instead, it was the handsomest man she'd ever seen, and she took the opportunity to watch him the way she had that night in the hospital when she'd caught him sleeping in the chair next to her bed. The way he was stretched out now, though, really showed how tall he was, and she couldn't help smiling at how relaxed he looked.

She noticed the open book lying on his chest, and she loved the idea that he was enjoying a series she did as well. For a few moments, she imagined sitting by that creek on his ranch on a regular basis, talking about the books they were reading. She couldn't imagine anything more perfect. Well, except for him returning the feelings that seemed to be building within her at an increasing speed. She suddenly wanted to scream at her grandmother for doing her best to burn that belief into her mind that the family into which she'd been born somehow made her lesser, at her mother for living her life in a way that gave supporting evidence Anna had seen with her own eyes.

But Anna didn't want to think that way anymore. She suspected a part of her had always resisted it. And yet, there was enough fear that she was wrong and Helena had been right that she struggled within her own mind.

Anna startled when Roman shifted and the book fell to the floor. He jerked awake at the resulting thump before she could move away.

"What's wrong?" he asked, instantly alert as he lowered his feet to the floor.

She held out a palm and waved off his concern. "Nothing. I'm sorry I woke you up."

He rubbed his hand over his face and shook his head as if trying to dispel that fog that lingered whenever waking suddenly from a deep sleep.

"No, it's okay." He spotted the book and lifted it from the floor. "I think this is the culprit."

She somehow remembered how to move her feet and took a few steps toward the kitchen. "Are you hungry? I'm surprised my growling stomach wasn't what woke you."

Or somehow sensing someone was staring at him as he slept.

Roman got to his feet and followed her. "You rest. I can

scrounge up something."

She didn't even think about it before she stopped and turned toward him. "You do realize I just slept for several hours, don't you?"

He glanced toward the window, as if he had no clue what time it was. That reminded her of her earlier thought.

"Why isn't Paige here?"

"She texted that she wasn't feeling well and asked if I minded staying with you tonight. I hope that's okay. I don't want you to feel weird about having a man in your house."

"No, it's fine." Which wasn't entirely true. The thought of him being there all night, just the two of them, made her entire being vibrate with nervous energy. "But truly, I'm okay to stay by myself."

He covered a yawn, making her realize that if he stayed she might actually be helping him more than her.

"But you're obviously too tired to drive, so you're welcome to the couch. Sorry it isn't more comfortable."

He laughed a little. "I've slept worse places."

"Somehow I doubt that."

"Really. I lost count of how many cricks I got in my neck from falling asleep at desks, sitting up in dorm beds, on park benches while studying during med school. I once woke up with my face smashed against a desk in the library and my best friend taking a picture of me to post on every social media platform known to man."

She laughed. "Tell me you weren't drooling, too."

"I can't."

Anna laughed even harder, more than she had in she couldn't remember how long.

"I'm glad that's still bringing amusement all these years later," he said.

She motioned toward the kitchen table. "Have a seat and I'll fix us something to eat."

"I can do it."

"I swear if you tell me to rest again, I'm going to stab you with the first poky object I find."

He held up his hands, palms out, in surrender. "Sorry. Hard to turn off the doctor."

"I do appreciate all the help you've given me, but I'm tired of Doctor Roman. I don't mind Friend Roman though."

He smiled in a way that made her insides start fluttering, as if he might be reading more into "friend" and didn't mind.

Though she was growing more determined to change her outlook on the possibilities her life could offer, she still believed she had to be careful to not project what part of her wanted to see rather than what was actually in front of her. To hopefully get her feelings under control, she turned her back to him and went to the refrigerator.

"How do you feel about chicken quesadillas?"

"Sounds good."

Over the course of the next few minutes, she used the rotisserie chicken Paige had brought with the groceries yesterday to make some easy, quick quesadillas while Roman scrolled through messages on his phone. When she slid the plates with the food onto the table, he set the phone aside, face-down. Were the messages private patient information? Or was he seeing someone? He hadn't said anything about dating anyone, but why would he? They might be friends now, but she didn't think they were to the point where they discussed love lives. Thank goodness, because she didn't want to hear about his and she had nothing to share.

"Justin sent me the final tally for what the trail ride earned." He gave her a figure she hadn't expected, but then she had no idea how much it had cost to take part. "As soon as we announced the money would be going to you, the number of people participating doubled."

She dropped the fork that had been halfway to her mouth back to her plate.

"I told you people liked you," he said.

"I...I don't know what to say. Or how to pay everyone back."

"You don't have to pay everyone back. That's the point." He reached across the table and placed his hand over hers. "Just keep being yourself. The person you are without effort is why people want to help you."

Damn if tears didn't pool in her eyes. "I had no idea. I mean, I don't think I'm an ogre, but I...I'm just stunned, I guess."

"You're very easy to like, Anna."

She met his gaze and, no, she hadn't been imagining his interest earlier. But was it just some sort of empathy doctor thing? Or could the son of the first family of Logan Springs really be interested in her? She didn't think she was ugly, but she just wasn't the type of woman she ever pictured with any of the McQueens. After all, Justin was marrying the owner of a pharmaceutical company. Sure, Wes played the field, but when he settled down, his partner would likely be stunning.

And Roman? On top of everything else, he was a doctor. As much as she might want him to, she found it difficult to picture him choosing a stereotypical shy librarian.

"Thanks," she said, retrieving her hand as if she needed it to eat. "You are, too."

She had to steer the conversation a different direction or she wasn't going to make it through the rest of the night. Before she could think of a topic, however, Roman spoke again.

"We can put the money into your bank account on Monday morning," he said. "That way you can start getting things you need, like a car."

"That will likely be down the list. I can walk to work since the weather is nice. That way I can start chipping away at the medical bills first." She looked up and saw the look on his face, like he wanted to say something but didn't know if he should. "What?"

"The medical bills are going to be substantial."

"I'm aware. But I need to whittle down those bills as fast as I can. I've never carried debt, not even for college, and I hate that I have to now."

His expression shifted to worry. "I hate the idea of you

overdoing things so quickly after your injuries."

"I'm not a fool. I won't do anything that might put me right back in the hospital, racking up even more bills."

"I know you're a smart woman, but you're also stubbornly independent."

"So you've said."

"Sorry, I don't mean to offend you."

She tilted her head slightly, trying to figure out this man before her. "It must be exhausting worrying about everyone so much all the time."

"See, that's the thing. Normally, I don't. I care, but I also know how to distance myself when necessary. But there is something about you, Anna Kenner, that brings out my protective instincts."

Words failed her. Utterly, completely failed her. So she almost knocked over her chair getting up from the table and carrying her dishes to the sink. She wished she could temporarily disappear into another realm long enough to get the frantic beating of her heart under control, to think of some way to respond to his revelation. Did he mean that as a friend? As more than a friend? It seemed like the latter, but she was really awful at reading signs from men. That took practice, of which she had woefully little.

While part of her wanted to rejoice that this man who had been filling so many of her thoughts might be attracted to her, another part wanted to strangle Paige for putting her in this situation. Because there wasn't a doubt in her mind that her friend felt just fine and was likely sitting on her couch eating popcorn, smiling at the mere thought of her matchmaking machinations.

✪

HE'D MADE A mistake. Or had he? He was a big believer in telling the truth. His mom had taught him that from a young age, deciding never to hide the truth of his cancer and his prognosis from him. When doctors had wanted to talk to her privately, she'd refused, saying he was the one sick and deserved to know what was going on. He always had that thought in the back of his mind as he dealt with patients and their families, and he tried to always employ the same principle in his life outside work. He'd held his feelings inside as long as he could, but Anna's reaction had him doubting his timing.

And yet he wasn't sorry he'd said the words. It was out there now, not bouncing around inside him looking for a way to escape. But based on her reaction, he had no idea how to proceed. What did he even want?

He realized he actually knew what he wanted—to ask her out on a date. But he suspected if he asked her out now, the answer would be a kind but resounding no. Best to tread lightly and see if being her friend would lead to her being receptive of more.

"So what do you and Paige normally do when she stays over?"

"Talk, watch TV."

"Let me guess. You like mysteries on TV, too."

She glanced over her shoulder at him before returning her attention to the sink. "That's more deductive reasoning than a guess." She gestured across the living room. "Judging by the fact that you found my bookshelf, you know I wasn't kidding about liking mysteries."

"So why mysteries?"

She shrugged. "I just like trying to figure out all the clues. I like puzzles, too, so I guess it's a theme."

"You got any?"

"What? Puzzles?"

"Yeah."

"Roman, you don't want to do a puzzle."

"You don't know that. I might be the puzzle king." He breathed a bit easier when she snort-laughed.

"Just find something that looks good."

Though he wanted to continue talking to her, he headed for the living room and clicked on the TV.

"I don't even know what most things are anymore," he said. "I watch sports and the occasional movie, but other than hearing people at work talking about shows I'm clueless."

Anna came into the room and took the remote from him, the brief brush of her fingers against his making him want to pull her close. When she sank onto the couch, he sent out a silent thanks and sat beside her. He noticed a momentary stiffening of her posture, but then she relaxed enough that he realized she must have forced it.

"Do I scare you?" Hell, why had he said that out loud?

"No, why?"

He shrugged. "I don't know. I just seem to make you anxious."

"I'm fine. So, have you ever seen *Longmire?*"

She wasn't telling the truth, but he wasn't going to push her. He had to be fine with baby steps.

"No. I've heard it's good though."

"I think you'll really like it."

"But you've seen it? I doubt the mysteries will be intriguing if you already know who the bad guy is in every episode."

"It's very re-watchable."

"All right, let's watch an episode."

But as the show began to play, Roman had a hard time concentrating on the characters. Instead, he watched as Anna continued to sit on the edge of the couch, leaning forward. After several minutes, he couldn't stand it anymore.

"I don't bite, you know. I'm fairly sure it's against the Hippocratic Oath."

"I didn't say you did."

"You didn't have to. Your posture said it for you."

She hesitated for a few seconds but then scooted back and relaxed. To help her, he managed to keep his hands to himself and his attention focused forward. As one episode flowed into another, he sensed Anna relaxing more next to him. And to his surprise, he found himself getting caught up in the stories and characters on the screen.

When the second episode finished, Anna asked, "What do you think?"

"I think we could use some popcorn before the next episode."

"As luck would have it, I have some."

He smiled as she hopped up and headed toward the kitchen, not only because she seemed to be more relaxed around him now. He was also glad to see her acting so normal. Just looking at her, no one would be able to tell how bad of an accident she'd been in, how he'd worried that she might not wake up. That thought made something knot tightly in his middle.

"So you liked mysteries even as a kid, the Nancy Drews and all that?" he asked as she threw a bag of popcorn in the microwave.

"Yeah. I flew through every kid mystery series the library had."

"I remember Mom read me some of the old Hardy Boys books when I was sick."

"Probably the same books I read."

When she came back to the couch with the bowl of piping hot popcorn, the scent making her house smell like a movie theater, she didn't immediately grab the remote to start the next episode. Instead, she pulled one leg up under her and faced him.

"I can't remember. How long were you sick?"

"Two years."

"That must have been scary."

174

"Not going to lie. It was. I tried to not make a big deal of it because I could see how scared Mom and Dad were, but I was a kid. Sometimes I'd get mad or cry because I couldn't go riding with Justin and Wes."

"How old were you? I remember it was elementary school. I might have been in kindergarten."

"I was in first grade when I was diagnosed. Got the clean bill of health right before Christmas in third."

"I'm sorry you had to go through that."

She sounded absolutely genuine, like if she could go back in time and prevent his suffering she would. And it didn't surprise him one bit. That was just the kind of person she was.

"I remember everyone at school signed a big card for me. I still have it somewhere. Wonder if your signature is on there."

"Probably in fat crayon with half the letters backward."

He laughed a little at that. "I doubt it. I suspect you have known the proper way to make letters since birth."

"I'm not sure how to take that."

"As a compliment."

She lifted an eyebrow as if she wasn't quite sure he was being honest.

He lifted his hand and extended three fingers upward. "Scout's honor."

"Were you ever a Boy Scout?"

"Well, no, but the meaning fits."

She scooted around to face the TV and started episode

three.

"I just realized," he said, a few minutes in. "That's the girl from *Battlestar Galactica*, isn't it?"

"Yes. So you do watch some TV. Or did. That show's about a decade old now, counting from the end of its run."

"I had more free time then."

As the minutes continued to tick by, they made their way through three more episodes while consuming the bowl of popcorn and periodically pausing the show to discuss what else a certain actor had been in. Roman realized he hadn't had such a fun evening in a long time, even if he couldn't indulge his desire to wrap his arm around Anna and pull her close. For now, this easy camaraderie would have to suffice.

CHAPTER TWELVE

DISORIENTED. THAT WAS the word that came to mind as Anna woke to find herself staring at her living room instead of the familiar environs of her bedroom. She blinked a few times before reality hit like a sudden wave. Not only had she fallen asleep on the couch, but she'd also somehow ended up leaning against Roman's shoulder.

A lonely little voice in her head wanted so much to snuggle in closer, but she was afraid of his reaction. Hanging out and watching TV was one thing. Even sharing deeply personal memories didn't seem as intimate as curling up together would be.

Unable to tell if he was asleep, she eased away from his shoulder thinking how she'd not been that close to a guy since a four-month romance in college. Her few dates since then hadn't exactly set the world on fire either.

"Hey," he said, his voice thick with sleep.

She stood. "Stretch out and go back to sleep."

He opened his eyes a fraction. "What time is it?"

"Middle of the night. See you in the morning."

As she started to step away, he surprised her by taking her hand. "Thanks. This was nice."

It was so much more than nice, but she simply gave him a quick smile and a nod before retreating to the safety of her bedroom. If she didn't get away from him, she was afraid her unspoken desire to feel his arms around her was going to overwhelm her common sense.

When she crawled into her bed, she hugged her pillow the way she'd wanted to wrap her arms around Roman's warm body. Earlier, she couldn't believe she was spending a Saturday night binge watching TV with Roman McQueen, a man who made her pulse race as if it was a rocket taking off for space. But how many times had she touched him today? The holding of hands had been really nice on its own. To wake up next to him and to have him not seem to mind was just... Despite her grasp of the English language, she couldn't think of a word to fully explain how she was feeling—sort of like she'd experienced a full-on miracle.

She could never tell Paige about this because her friend would read way more into the evening than was really there. After all, she and Paige had fallen asleep watching TV on more than one occasion. This was no different.

Except you didn't want to press yourself as close to Paige as humanly possible.

Her cheeks heated so much that she buried her face in the pillow, as if there was someone in the room with her who could bear witness to her embarrassing thoughts.

She didn't sleep. Couldn't. Instead, her mind kept replaying all of their interactions, all the times her body had made contact with his in any way. As she thought about the bits of his past he'd shared with her, she thanked God that he had survived his cancer. That he'd been able to grow into a man with such caring and compassion a very big part of who he was.

After she saw the first light of dawn creeping in through her windows, she felt her eyes getting heavy again. She should really get up so her sleep schedule wouldn't be totally out of whack considering she was going back to work the next day. Despite her best intentions, however, she drifted off.

The sound of the front door jerked her awake. Was that Paige coming to relieve Roman? For the first time since they'd become friends when she hired Paige at the library, Anna wasn't in the mood to see her friend. Though she knew Roman couldn't stay forever, she had looked forward to at least having coffee together before he headed home.

But maybe this was for the best, especially since she wasn't sure she could hide her embarrassment at having slept propped up next to him the night before.

After brushing her teeth and running a comb through her hair, she made her way to the living room only to find it empty. No Roman. No Paige. Though she'd told them both she was okay to be alone, she hadn't expected it to happen quite so suddenly and without even a goodbye. She crossed to the living room window and looked outside. Her driveway sat empty, and suddenly her heart felt the same. She bit her lip at the idea that once Roman had come fully awake, he'd wanted to make his exit before having to face her again.

Maybe he'd just had some sort of medical emergency, a patient in need, and hadn't wanted to wake her.

Blinking against stupid tears, she trudged into the kitchen to make coffee. She supposed it was time to get used to her normal state of being again. During all that time in the hospital and the rehab facility, being back in the quiet, familiar space of her home was what she'd said she wanted. But after last night...well, now it felt emptier than it ever had, emptier even than the days right after she'd been forced to put her grandmother in the nursing home.

She'd just pulled the coffee out of the cabinet when she heard a vehicle pull up in her driveway, one that did not sound like Paige's little car. Her heart thumping wildly, she glanced outside to see Roman getting out of his truck. She hurried back to the kitchen, not wanting him to know she'd been watching him.

The front door opened quietly to reveal Roman holding a big paper bag, the kind that the Big Sky Café used for takeout orders.

He looked startled to see her standing there looking at him. "Did I wake you when I left?"

"Yes, but that's okay. I needed to get up so I'm not up all night tonight."

He nodded toward the coffeemaker. "No need to fire that up. I brought coffee with breakfast."

"You didn't have to do that."

"It's partially self-serving. I figure I need to fuel up if I'm going to watch the rest of season one today."

"You're…not going home?"

"I will if you want me to, but I had a good time last night. I have nothing on my to-do list for today if you're game for some more binge watching."

Part of her was freaking out while another part was dancing with joy. She began to consider that more than friendship was going on here. Did he reciprocate her feelings? Or was this really no different than the girls' weekends she and Paige had on occasion? She wished she could read his thoughts just for a moment to know for certain.

"Sure." It was better than whatever she would have eventually gotten around to. Way better.

"You want to eat at the table or the couch?"

She motioned toward the couch. "Might as well dive right in."

As he pulled containers out of the large bag and placed them on the coffee table, it began to feel like an endless array of clowns exiting one of those little clown cars.

"Are we expecting half of Logan Springs to come over and watch TV?"

"I didn't know what you liked."

One of the questions bouncing around in her head spilled out. "Roman, why are you doing this?"

He stopped retrieving takeout containers and met her gaze. "Because last night was the most fun I've had in a long time. I love my work and helping people, but it doesn't leave a lot of time for pure fun."

"You could be spending time with your family. You

could watch TV at your own home without splurging on half of the food in Lena's restaurant."

"Eating chips and watching TV alone doesn't have quite the same allure."

She couldn't move, stunned into silence. The sound of *allure* on his lips sent want crackling along her skin like flames consuming dry tinder.

She forced her gaze to the food containers. "There any French toast in there?"

"Yes, ma'am."

Within a couple of minutes, she was enjoying delicious French toast, hot coffee, and watching one of her favorite shows alongside the handsomest man to ever stroll through her life. She kept expecting to wake up, for everything to be a dream, but she didn't. Instead, over the course of the day they watched the rest of season one while devouring the remainder of the breakfast spread he'd bought.

In between episodes, they talked about their respective years at college, their work, the latest plans for Justin and Melody's wedding, and what seemed like a million other little things. By late in the afternoon, Anna had come to realize just how much more full her life could be if she let it.

But not in the way that she really wanted. Her grandmother's warnings echoed in her mind, but she shoved them away with no small amount of mental anger. This might very well have been the best weekend of her life, but she and Roman were still just friends. Maybe there was something different bubbling under the surface, but neither of them had taken a step across the invisible line between friendship and more than friendship.

"I guess I should get going," he said as the credits rolled on the final episode of season one. "I've hogged enough of your weekend."

"You haven't." She already missed him and he hadn't even left. "It was fun. Thank you, for everything."

"Anytime. I mean, I have to see the rest of the seasons at some point." He grinned at her in a way that threatened to melt everything in her that was female.

She watched as he hesitated, almost as if he wanted to say something else, before he headed for the door. To her surprise, he turned when he reached it and gave her a quick hug that still had her feeling breathless as he drove up the street and back to his normal life.

How she'd wanted that hug to last longer, to go on forever. In those fleeting moments, she'd been able to feel a hint of just how well made Roman was under his clothes, and she'd almost asked him to stay. But she'd bitten down on those words, still unsure the best move to find out if there could be more, if she wasn't just fooling herself into seeing something that wasn't there.

As if Paige could read Anna's thoughts, her best friend picked that moment to text her.

How's your weekend going?

She followed the question with a winking emoji.

You're not sick, are you?

Of course I am. ::CoughCough::

I'll see you in the morning.

You're going to leave me hanging?

Anna didn't respond.

ROMAN CONSIDERED BYPASSING the ranch altogether. He'd left nothing there that he had to have before the next time he visited, but he also knew his family. The longer he waited before showing his face, the more they were going to tease him. He'd already gotten a couple of smart-aleck texts from Wes, who couldn't seem to help himself.

When he stepped out of his truck in front of his family's home, he acted as if nothing was out of the ordinary. Because, really, it wasn't. He'd spent the night at a friend's house. Each of his brothers had done the same thing at various points in their lives. Though he might have had thoughts of more over the course of the past twenty-four hours, he and Anna were only friends.

Even if when she'd fallen asleep beside him, resting her head on his shoulder, he'd wanted to pull her fully into his arms, to stretch out on that couch with her, to make her feel safe and protected and... He tried not to let the last thought form, but there was no denying it. He was falling for Anna Kenner. He just didn't know how best to see if he could take things further with her.

"I never in my life thought I'd see this one do the walk of shame," Wes said as Roman walked through the front door.

"Oh, leave him alone," Melody said as she came over and gave him a hug. "I think it's wonderful. I couldn't think of two nicer people."

"We're just friends," he tried to claim but was met with a mixture of laughter and knowing looks. Even his dad snorted.

Leaving the lot of them behind, he went to the room he'd used all his life and gathered up his clothes.

"You might want to take a shower," Wes yelled down the hall. "You still smell like trail ride."

"Bite me," he called back, which only elicited more laughter.

When he had all his stuff bagged up, he turned to leave only to find Justin standing in the doorway.

"What?"

His big brother gestured with his thumb toward the living room. "Ignore that idiot. I'm with Melody. You and Anna seem like a good match."

"Nobody seems to believe me when I say nothing happened."

"But did you want it to?"

He felt weird talking to Justin about this despite how he'd encouraged him to make things work with Melody. With a sigh, he sank onto the edge of the bed.

"I think so, but she's more skittish than a newborn colt."

"She's always been on the shy side."

"It feels like more than that."

"What do you mean?"

"I don't know. Almost like she thinks too much or something."

"You'll figure it out. You're the smartest person I know."

"Don't let Melody hear you say that."

"She'd agree with me."

It surprised Roman just how much his brother's words meant to him.

"You've overcome a lot in your life," Justin said. "And you've worked harder than anyone I know to get where you are. You deserve to have all the happiness in the world. If Anna is part of that, I hope you find a way to convince her and she feels the same. For the record, Melody thinks she does."

"What makes her think that?"

"Something about how Anna looked at you yesterday. It's one of those female intuition things. Don't ask me to explain it."

Roman laughed. "They should have a class on that in med school, but they don't."

"Women can be complex, but when you find the right one you don't even mind."

Roman thought about what Justin had said all the way back to Livingston. When he walked into his house, it hit him how quiet it was, how empty compared to the homey feel of Anna's. As he dropped his bag, he wanted nothing more than to return to his truck and drive right back to Logan Springs, confess his feelings to Anna, and hope she reciprocated.

But common sense told him not to blow what might be his only chance. Though it might feel like torture, he had to take things slowly.

✪

IT CAME AS no surprise that Paige was waiting for her with an expectant look on her face when Anna arrived at the library the next morning.

"So?"

Paige didn't have to say anything else for Anna to know what she was asking.

"We binge watched the first season of *Longmire*."

Paige continued to stare. "And?"

"We ate popcorn."

"You...are...killing...me."

Anna couldn't help grinning. "Good. You're nosy."

"Come on, was there any kissing involved?"

Anna tossed her purse in her desk drawer and looked up at Paige. "Honestly, why would there be any kissing? Do you go around kissing your friends?"

"I would if they looked like Roman McQueen."

Anna winced as she glanced past Paige into the main part of the library. She did not need the gossip to start churning.

"Roman and I are friends, nothing more." Right?

Paige sighed. "Well, that's disappointing. You two would make beautiful babies."

Anna dropped into her chair. "I don't know what has gotten into you, but you need to stop."

"Do you not like him?"

"Of course I like him. Who wouldn't?"

"You know what I mean."

"Paige, I love you, but you need to drop it. There is no world in which Roman and I would work as a couple." It felt like a lie on her tongue, and yet it felt safer to retreat into that mindset.

"That's your grandmother talking."

"She's not totally wrong."

"She's completely full of crap."

Before Anna could recover from the forcefulness of Paige's words and respond, a patron required her friend's help at the front desk.

Anna tried to bury herself in work, but between pondering what Paige had said, her own fears about misreading Roman's interest, and a steady stream of well-wishers welcoming her back to the library, she got pitiful little done on her first day back.

The one good thing was that she wasn't totally exhausted as the end of the workday approached.

Her phone dinged and she absentmindedly picked it up. Her heart rate sped up when she saw it was a text from Roman, and she looked out her open office door as if somehow Paige would be able to tell.

One of the nurses in the office is selling her car. What do you think?

He attached a photo of a cute little silver crossover.

She's moving to New York and doesn't need a car anymore, he continued.

It looks nice, but I can't buy a car yet.

It's a good price, and Justin had all the proceeds from the trail ride deposited in your account this morning.

He had? She thought about the bills stacking up and the ones that hadn't yet landed in her mailbox. The truth was she might need a second job to pay them off, and for that she might very well need a car.

And in order to go look at this possibility, she was going to have to make peace with Paige and ask for a ride.

Melody is coming through Livingston to go to the airport in about an hour. You can catch a ride with her.

What if I don't buy the car?

Then I'll take you home.

I don't want you to have to do that.

You worry too much.

She really did need a car, even if the thought of getting back behind the wheel made her stomach churn. And if she was being honest with herself, she wanted to see him again. Still, she stared at the screen of her phone before managing to reply with a simple OK.

"Are you mad at me?"

She looked up to see Paige had entered the office at some point.

"No. I just don't like to be pushed out of my comfort zone."

"I'm sorry if this weekend was really uncomfortable. I just want you to be happy, and I honestly worry that you won't reach out and grab that happiness when it shows up for the taking."

"I know you care. I appreciate it, I really do. You've been a lifesaver since the accident. And I can't lie and say I'm not interested in Roman. But I also have to think about this logically. I've known Roman since we were kids. Not super well, but enough to chat a bit when we see each other. It's a giant leap to think we'd suddenly fall in love and live happily ever after."

Though the thought of such a thing filled her with a burst of blinding joy that made her wonder if continuing to deliberately see him was such a good idea. If she let herself get too close, it was going to hurt all the worse if she found out she'd been wrong about him and he ended up with someone else.

"It doesn't mean it couldn't happen. All I ask is that you stop letting Helena's outlook on life be yours. She ended up bitter and alone. I don't want that to happen to you. You have too beautiful of a soul for that to happen."

Tears pooled in Anna's eyes, and love for her friend propelled her to her feet. She gathered Paige in a tight hug.

"Thank you for being such a good friend."

"You make it easy," Paige said. "Well, most of the time."

Anna laughed.

Paige stepped back out of the embrace. "Need a ride home?"

"Actually, Melody Redmond is giving me a ride to Livingston to look at a car."

"Oh?"

"Roman texted that someone in his office is selling her car because she's moving to New York and doesn't need it."

Paige appeared to try to hide her smile but failed miserably. "That's good. Have fun *car shopping*," she said as she backed toward the door using air quotes.

"Be careful or I might fire you."

Paige just laughed at the baseless threat.

After making sure the library was empty of patrons, she turned off most of the lights and headed outside. After locking the front door, she sat on the bench next to the walkway. She planned to use the time to once again convince herself this was a good idea, that she wasn't just setting herself up for a massive disappointment down the road. But she didn't have more than fifteen seconds to think before Melody pulled up to the curb.

"Hey, there!" Melody said when Anna opened the passenger door. "I'm so glad to have company for part of my trip."

"Are you flying to Atlanta?" Anna asked as Melody pulled back out onto the street.

"Yeah, duty calls. Meetings, meetings and more meetings."

Anna wondered if some of those meetings had to do with Melody's stepsister's upcoming trial. It was a marvel that Melody could be so happy considering last winter her evil stepsister had tried to have her killed. But Justin had helped thwart that effort and won Melody's heart in the process. It was a modern-day fairy tale when she thought about it.

"How are the wedding plans coming?"

Melody spent the next several minutes going over the details with infectious enthusiasm.

"You're invited, of course. I don't think I would have gotten through those first few months here if not for your book recommendations. They kept my mind off of things I couldn't change."

"I'm happy they helped. But I'd say that pushing through those tough months worked out well in the end." Anna was afraid if Melody smiled any wider, she was going to pull a muscle.

"So, how are you doing? I hear today was your first day back at work."

"Fine. I was very lucky things turned out as well as they did."

"I hope they find the person who caused your wreck. As you can imagine, I'm a bit militant against people hurting others."

"I hope they find him, too, so it doesn't happen again."

"Have you remembered anything else?"

Anna shook her head. "No."

"Maybe it'll come back eventually. But in the meantime, it's good to see you doing so well. I was worried the trail ride would be too much for you, but you seemed to enjoy it."

"I did. Even living here my entire life, I sometimes forget how beautiful it is. Sometimes you just need to look at things from a different perspective."

"You're right about that."

Something about the tone of Melody's response made Anna think she was talking about something other than the view of the snow-capped mountains. And she had a strong suspicion she knew what—or rather, who—it was.

"Roman seemed to have a good time, too. He works so hard we don't get to see him that much. But I didn't hear him mention work once on Saturday."

Yep, Melody was definitely playing matchmaker, but Anna was willing to give her a pass because she was caught up in all things romantic while planning her wedding. Plus, she didn't know Anna's background the way Paige did. Even Paige didn't know everything.

As they rolled into the southern end of Livingston, Melody grew quiet. It hit Anna that they were passing the spot where the police had rescued Melody from her kidnappers, where she'd been taken away from Justin and hadn't known if she'd ever see him again.

Anna searched for something to say, but she kept coming up blank. Thankfully, within a couple of minutes they were pulling up in front of the medical building where Roman and Dr. Mills shared a practice.

"Thanks for the ride. Hope your trip goes well."

"You're welcome, and thank you."

Anna started to open her door.

"Anna?"

She turned her attention back toward the other woman.

"I know this isn't any of my business, and you can tell me to butt out and I will. But I just wanted to say that I think there might be something between you and Roman. You're two of the kindest people I've ever met, so I'd be thrilled if that was the case."

"We're just friends." How many times was she going to have to say that, both to others and to herself? Maybe one day she'd actually believe it.

"Justin and I started out as just friends. Something to keep in mind."

The way she smiled, Anna couldn't even be upset at her. But she also didn't commit to anything because believing in this particular dream felt like she might be setting herself up for heartache. She'd seen what loving someone who didn't love her back had done to her mother, and she'd sworn at a young age to not go down that same path.

"Okay." It seemed the easiest and least committal way to exit from the conversation.

She waved as Melody drove off, heading to Bozeman and her flight. Anna took a deep, fortifying breath before she headed inside the building.

"Hey, there," Dr. Mills said as she nearly bumped into

him coming out of the clinic's small pharmacy. "How are you feeling?"

"Pretty good, thanks to you and Dr. White."

"I hear you've come to check out Andrea's car," he said as they walked side by side down the corridor.

"Yeah. Until they invent teleportation, I need wheels."

"Oh, wouldn't that be nice? I could just pop over to Seattle to see the Mariners play and be home in time to go to bed."

When they reached the doctors' office, she started to head into the waiting area.

"Come this way," he said, indicating another entrance he opened with the swipe of his ID through a card reader.

She followed him past a few exam rooms.

"Look who I found," he said as she spotted Roman.

Damn if her pulse didn't start racing again. Would she ever be able to see him without that happening? Thank goodness her reaction wasn't visible. At least she hoped it wasn't. That would be mortifying.

"Hey," he said, and the way he smiled at her made her wonder if Melody might be right.

For the first time, she truly considered ignoring every single thing her grandmother had ever taught her about managing expectations.

Chapter Thirteen

Roman realized he'd been staring at Anna a bit too long when he noticed how Andrew wasn't even trying to hide his knowing smile.

"Let me get Andrea," he said just as the nurse walked out of an exam room.

"Andrea, this is Anna."

"Oh, hey," Andrea said. "It's good to meet you. I hope you like the car. If I can get rid of it quickly, that's the last big thing I have to do other than, you know, actually move. Let me grab my keys."

As the two women headed outside, Roman tagged along, having seen his last patient of the day.

"Roman says you're moving to New York."

"Yeah. My college roommate lives there. She's an actress and has been in some off-Broadway shows. Her brother is a doctor at Mount Sinai and helped me get a job there. I can't wait. It's so different than here, something going on all the time. So much to do and see. Have you ever been?"

"No, but it sounds nice."

Really? He didn't figure Anna for someone who would like the pace of a city that size. He wanted to ask Andrea to stop talking before she convinced Anna to head to the Big Apple, too.

"This is it," Andrea said. "Take her for a spin and see what you think."

"You're not coming?" Anna asked.

"No, I have a few things to finish up inside. Take Doc with you. He can let you back in the building when you're done."

When Andrea headed inside, Roman noticed Anna staring at the car without making a move to get in.

"You okay?"

She slowly shifted her gaze to him. "I'm not sure I can do it."

"Buy the car? I think Andrea is willing to come down some on the price to get rid of it."

She shook her head. "No. That's not what I mean. I feel nauseated just thinking about getting behind the wheel."

"That's natural after being in a bad accident. But you have to face it or the fear will just get worse, possibly debilitating."

She pressed her palm to her forehead.

"You can do this. I have complete faith in you."

She still looked nervous, but to her credit she opened the driver's side door and slipped behind the wheel. He buckled himself into the passenger seat. When she drove out of the parking lot, she went slowly, like a teenager with a freshly minted driver's license. Or one of his older patients with a slower reaction time than when they were younger.

After she'd made her way up and down a couple of streets, he pointed south. "Head for the interstate."

"It's okay. I can tell the car is fine."

"You've barely gotten it above fifteen miles per hour. Trust me, okay?"

For a moment, he thought she would refuse. But then she made the necessary turn. As she approached the on ramp, however, she slowed down.

"Andrea probably doesn't want me taking her car this far."

"I promise she won't mind."

Despite looking unsure, he took it as a good sign that she trusted him enough to drive onto the ramp. It took her a couple of miles, but she gradually approached a decent speed for interstate travel. Though he noticed her hands were gripped tightly around the steering wheel.

"How's it feel?"

"Okay."

He heard the anxiety in her voice, and he hoped he wasn't making a mistake as he told her to make a U-turn up ahead.

"That's illegal."

"No one else is around, and I won't tell if you don't. Besides, the next exit is more than ten miles down the road."

She looked ahead and then in the rearview mirror before quickly executing the turn. Once she had headed back toward Livingston, she let out an audible breath of relief. He watched her expression and saw the moment she realized this was the stretch of highway she'd been on the day of her accident.

"Just breathe," he said.

"I seriously feel like I'm going to throw up."

"Well, if you do that, you'll have no choice but to buy the car."

She glanced over at him as if he'd lost his mind, but in the next instant she laughed. It was shaky but real. He hated to kill it by what he intended to ask of her next.

Another mile down the road, he pointed to the emergency lane. "Pull over down here."

"Where?" The word had just left her mouth when she saw the first of the skid marks, still visible despite the weeks that had passed since her accident.

She pulled off the road and came to a stop. She yelped when an eighteen-wheeler passed, its wake buffeting the smaller vehicle.

Roman reached over and placed his hand atop one of hers on the steering wheel. "It's okay."

"Why are we here?"

"Because I think facing things head-on is the best way to move past them."

"How is looking at where I wrecked going to change anything?"

"You're going to have to go to Bozeman again at some point. Better to get this moment over with now, when you've got someone with you."

She stared at him as if she couldn't understand why he'd

do such a thing, why he would care so much. If she only knew. But one emotional overload at a time.

He got out of the car and came around to her side, where she still sat. After checking that there was no approaching traffic, he opened her door and extended his hand. She took a visible deep breath before unbuckling her seat belt and placing her hand in his. He didn't let her go as she got out, as he closed the door and escorted her to the spot where the skid marks on the pavement gave way to visible tracks through the grass beside the road.

When Anna saw the trail her car had cut while tumbling down the hill, she stopped and squeezed his hand even tighter.

"Oh, my God," she said, barely audible. "How did I survive that?"

"You were very lucky."

She wiped at a tear that had escaped, and he wanted so much to pull her into his arms. But he had to keep reminding himself to take things slowly. Right now, what was important was for her to fully accept what had happened and move past it.

"I don't even know how long I was down there."

"From all the evidence that was pieced together, we believe less than an hour."

"I...I want to thank the couple who found me."

"I'm sure you can get their names from the sheriff's department. I believe they're from Minnesota."

He stayed quiet as Anna continued to stare down the

embankment, at the broken saplings and crushed vegetation, the occasional piece of torn metal or plastic that hadn't been cleared away by the tow truck driver. He would allow her all the time she needed.

She shifted her gaze to their surroundings further afield, the untouched trees and mountains.

"Hard to believe I almost died here."

The thought of that happening caused a pain in his chest.

"I'm glad that didn't happen."

She looked at him with that curious expression again. But before he could give in to his desire to erase the distance between them and kiss her, she lowered her gaze.

"We better get back before Andrea thinks I've absconded with her car."

When he felt her pulling her hand from his, he relaxed his grip. This time was all about her and what she needed. He had a feeling in his gut that she'd not had someone make her the center of anything in their life.

As she pulled off I-90 a few minutes later, driving more normally than when they'd headed out, he glanced over at her.

"So, what do you think?" He gestured to indicate the vehicle.

"I like it. I'm going to take it."

"Great."

Andrea was so thrilled to sell the car that she not only gave Anna an enthusiastic hug, but also a gift card to a local restaurant she said she didn't have time to use.

"Isn't that what I gave out to the staff last Christmas?" he asked.

Andrea looked sheepish. "What can I say? I'm a busy person. And forgetful."

Once the money had exchanged hands and Andrea had signed over the title, Anna looked at the car keys in her hand as if she couldn't figure out how they'd gotten there.

"We should go have dinner to celebrate," he said. "I skipped lunch and am starving."

"Why'd you skip lunch?"

"Patients to see. Paperwork to do. Drug reps to meet."

"Don't you just want to go home?"

"If I go home, I have to cook for myself. I'd rather have someone else do it." Not to mention he wanted to spend more time with her.

"Good point. I think I agree with you."

"You pick. My treat."

"No, we only go if I use this," she said, holding up the gift card. "You've already done too much for me."

"There's a limit on how much one friend can do for another?"

"Yes." He must have looked surprised because she waved off her quick answer. "I mean, let me do something for you for a change."

If it meant getting to spend the evening with her, he wasn't going to argue about who picked up the bill—especially since it evidently hadn't dawned on her that he'd already done so by buying that gift card in the first place.

THEY AGREED TO meet at the restaurant, but on the way there Anna wondered if she should have just gone on home. Her emotions were still all tangled up after their drive to where she'd had her accident. At first she hadn't wanted to face it, but when she had she'd experienced the most overwhelming sense of gratitude. It was so powerful that she'd nearly laid all her feelings bare there on the side of the interstate. She couldn't even fully explain why what he'd done had made something feel freer inside of her than she'd ever felt.

When she arrived, Roman was already standing outside the entrance waiting for her. After parking, she simply sat and stared at him for a moment, appreciating just how gorgeous of a man he was—inside and out.

His smile as she approached him made her insides do that flippy motion she was getting used to when around him. He held the door open for her but paused inside the door when another woman stepped toward them.

"Fancy meeting you here," the pretty blonde said, giving Anna a quick, curious glance before returning her attention to Roman.

"Hey," he said before shooting a glance of his own toward Anna. "Anna, this is Kailee, one of my neighbors. Kailee, Anna is a friend from Logan Springs."

Anna wasn't the most experienced person when it came to romantic relationships, but there was no mistaking the relief on Kailee's face when Roman called Anna a friend. A rush of jealousy flooded Anna's body like adrenaline when coming face to face with a wild animal that could end you. And though her relationship with Roman had only progressed to friendship, in that moment she wanted to proclaim he was more.

"Nice to meet you," Kailee said. "How long have you two been friends?"

The truth was not long, not real friends, but before Anna could figure out how to answer Roman did instead.

"Since elementary school."

Anna missed the rest of the conversation between Roman and his way-too-pretty neighbor as his answer bounced around in her head. Surely his definition of friends was different than hers because while they'd known each other since elementary school, she didn't think the occasional greeting counted as true friendship. More like friendly acquaintances.

After they were seated and the waitress had delivered their menus, Anna found she couldn't concentrate on anything until she had an answer.

"Why did you tell Kailee that we'd been friends since elementary school?"

He looked confused by her question. "Because we have been."

"That's stretching it, don't you think? I doubt we'd said

a hundred words to each other over the course of our lives before I woke up in the hospital."

"That's an exaggeration."

"Is it? We didn't exactly move in the same circles."

He placed his menu on the table. "Logan Springs isn't really big enough to have cliques."

She actually laughed that he evidently believed that. "How many times did we hang out in school?"

"You didn't want to."

"What?"

"You were so quiet and shy that you didn't even come to my sixteenth birthday party."

She was getting more confused by the minute. "What are you talking about? I was never invited to a party."

"Yeah, you were, but your grandmother told my mom that you weren't comfortable in crowds."

It hit Anna what must have happened at the same time as the realization that she couldn't tell him the truth. She could only imagine how he'd react if she said, "Oh, she said that because she doesn't believe people on our social strata should mix with yours, and she didn't want to take the chance that I might like you and forget everything I've been taught my entire life."

She'd sound crazy and rightly so. Sitting across from her was the most amazing man whose actions said he liked spending time with her, and a part of her was still trying to figure out a way to keep enough protective distance between them.

"Well, that's true." At least that wasn't a lie. She had always felt uncomfortable in crowds. "But, um, thanks for inviting me."

"I invited everyone."

Oh. So it hadn't been specifically aimed at her at all. The fact that she'd thought maybe it had been, even for a moment, told her that this evening should probably end quickly.

And yet it didn't. Instead, one topic of conversation flowed into another. The main course flowed into dessert. Anna was surprised all over again by how easy it was to talk to him now. They laughed and teased and commiserated so much that she wondered if to those seated around them it appeared they were on a date. Because as the night progressed, it was even feeling more and more like that to her.

That should be her cue to leave, but she couldn't make herself take that step. She wanted to indulge in the feeling as long as it lasted.

"Did you ever want to be anything other than a librarian?" he asked.

She considered saying no, but it felt good to be open and honest with someone.

"For a long time, I had this crazy thought about writing mystery novels of my own."

"You totally should. As many as you've read, I bet you'd be great at it."

She shook her head. "I did try but the rejection letters came back so fast my mailbox almost spun around in circles."

"You don't seem like the type of person to quit so easily. Remember, I saw you during rehab."

She smiled at his attempt at humor. "I think maybe it was more me trying to solve the mystery in my own life than creating fictional ones."

That wasn't totally true. She still sometimes imagined seeing her name on the front of a book in a bookstore. Since she'd arrived home from rehab, she'd even re-read what she'd written before and was surprised that it wasn't as terrible as she remembered. The story might actually be salvageable.

But the real mystery in her life was the one she'd more often wanted to solve. There was that part of her that always imagined she could somehow figure out the identity of her father, that maybe he was out there somewhere wondering about her.

Roman reached across the table and laced his fingers with hers. "The identity of your father?"

She nodded, stricken by how easily he seemed to be able to read her.

"I need to get home," she said as she pushed back from the table after paying the bill.

"Me, too. Very long day tomorrow."

"Free clinic day?"

"Yeah."

"It's really kind of you to give of your time like that."

He shrugged. "I got into medicine to help people, and not everyone can afford to pay for that help."

When they stepped outside, instead of heading to his truck he fell into step beside her.

"I'm just parked across the street," she said.

"I know."

She couldn't very well refuse to let him walk wherever he wanted, but by the time they reached her new car her nerves were jumping like crazy. That feeling she'd had of this being a date had increased with each step. And when she turned to face him, he was closer than she realized and her breath caught.

"I had a nice time tonight," he said, then glanced downward toward her lips.

He couldn't be thinking what she was thinking, right?

"It was nice. Thanks for all your help today. It does feel good to have the freedom of mobility again." She lowered her gaze, staring at a button halfway down his shirt. "What you did, out where I wrecked... I don't know why, but I felt better afterward. So thank you for that, too. You're a good friend."

She gasped a little when his finger lightly touched underneath her chin and lifted it until she was looking at him. "What would you say if I told you I wanted to be more than friends?"

Words absolutely failed her. So did rational thought because as she stared up at him, she saw something that thrilled her. Something that kept her from moving as he seemed to silently ask permission for what she knew was coming next. In the next moment, his mouth descended toward hers.

When his lips touched hers, she thought she might explode with happiness. She kissed him back and it felt more wonderful than anything she'd experienced in her entire life.

And then she heard her grandmother's voice. "Don't be as stupid as your mother. Powerful men only want one thing from women, and when they get it they move on to the next conquest. There are no fairy-tale endings. That's just crap made up to sell books and movies."

Anna jerked away from Roman as if the memory of her grandmother's voice had burned her. Roman reached for her, but she stepped out of his reach.

"Are you okay?" he asked.

She nodded, feeling anything but okay. "I...I just need to get home. Good night, Roman. Thanks again."

She fumbled her keys but managed to get into her car and shut the door before Roman said anything else. Though she did her best not to make eye contact with him again, she failed. Just before pulling out of the lot, she glanced over and saw the confusion on his face. Before she could cave to the desire to get back out and tell him he'd done nothing wrong, that she'd enjoyed his kiss more than she could adequately express, that how much she'd enjoyed it scared her, she drove away into the night.

CHAPTER FOURTEEN

ANNA WAS ABOUT to take the first bite of the salad she didn't really want when Paige strolled into her office with her lunch bag, shutting the door behind her, and parked herself in the chair on the other side of the desk.

"Can I help you?" Anna asked, really not in the mood to help anyone at the moment, not after she'd run away from the single best moment of her life the night before. "And leave the door open. Someone might need help."

"Which Serena will provide," Paige responded, referencing one of their volunteers. "We are going to use this lunch break for you to tell me where your mind has been all morning. I mean, I can guess, but I'd like to hear you actually say it."

"I'm not in the mood, Paige."

"Explain. And you know you'll be better off to just tell me now instead of having me pester you every five minutes until you do. I pester because I love."

Though she didn't even have to guess how Paige would react, Anna pushed her lunch away and told her what had happened the night before.

"You are certifiably crazy," Paige said when Anna finished. "Seriously, a guy who is not only hot but also the nicest guy ever, and you pushed him away?"

"I know, I know. I'm completely crazy."

"Yep."

"It just caught me so off guard."

"Why? You two have been spending a lot of time together, and word is meaningful looks have been going both ways."

"It's so tempting to just let things happen, but I just don't know if I'm wired that way. What if I'm more interested than he is? You know me. I'm not the type of person to have something that's just casual."

"You're just scared and brainwashed, and I feel like I should knock some sense into you and I'm not a violent person."

"I don't want to end up like my mother, broken and lost and always wanting someone I can't have."

Paige threw up her hands. "But you *can* have Roman. In case you missed it, he kissed you. He made the first move."

She heard everything Paige said, wanted to believe it, but the doubts in her mind refused to vacate the premises. Logan Springs was a small town, and even though Roman lived in Livingston she would still have to see him occasionally if things didn't work out. She wasn't sure she could handle that.

Paige was staring at her as if she was waiting for Anna to suddenly change her mind. Anna started to speak, not entirely sure what she was going to say, but her cell phone ringing drew her attention. Where it sat atop her desk, both she and Paige could see it was Roman calling.

Paige pointed at the phone as she stood. "You like him. He likes you. Stop listening to the doubts. Take a chance at being truly happy."

Anna considered letting the call go to voice mail. She could later claim she'd been working and hadn't heard it. But that would just delay the inevitable.

"Hello," she said as Paige left her office.

"Hey," he said, then hesitated. "I wanted to call and make sure you're okay."

"Fine. Just working."

"Listen, I'm sorry if I took things too far last night."

"No need to apologize."

"But you looked scared when you left."

"Not scared," she said, knowing that was a big fat lie. How much she'd wanted to keep kissing him, to believe they could have a happily ever after, *had* scared her, not anything he'd done. "Surprised."

"Can I make it up to you? I had a nice time at dinner. We could do that again. Just dinner."

A memory of one of the arguments between her mom and grandmother chose that moment to surface. Her mother told Helena that she'd found someone new, that things were going to work out this time. Helena had told her daughter she was an idiot and they'd all be lucky if Anna didn't grow up to be just like her.

"I appreciate how kind and generous you've been."

Though it might feel like she was ripping her own heart out, she had to stop this before it went too far, beyond the point where she could conceivably recover when things ended. "But we're not suited to be anything more than friends."

Tears threatened and she lifted her gaze to the ceiling to keep them at bay. Silence from his end of the line made her want to yank back her words.

"Why?"

How could she convince him that she was right?

"You've taken a lot of time out of your schedule to help me, and you don't have to do that anymore. You're a man whose entire world revolves around his job." Somehow she sensed he was about to but in, to contradict her. Time for the nail in the coffin. "I can't come second in a man's life. So it's best if we just walk away now. I'm sorry if I made you think we could be more than friends."

"Anna—"

"Sorry, I've got to go. I have a patron waiting for help." The lie tasted bitter on her tongue. Her entire life tasted bitter.

ROMAN COULDN'T BELIEVE what he'd just heard. That hadn't sounded like Anna at all, and yet she'd been the one to say the words. After she'd told him how much she admired him for devoting so much time to helping people, today she'd used that as an excuse why they couldn't pursue anything more than friendship. It just didn't feel right, almost as if she was being forced to make that excuse by someone else.

He tossed his phone onto his desk and rubbed his hand over his face. He'd slept like garbage the night before and had to make a conscious effort all morning to not bite off the heads of any patients or staff.

There were plenty of times in his life when he wished he could turn back time and do something over in a different way, but never more so than the previous night. He'd evidently read Anna completely wrong. It felt as if they'd grown even closer over dinner, and he'd thought he'd seen desire in her eyes too as he lowered his mouth to kiss her. And he knew he hadn't imagined her kissing him back. But she'd changed her mind, and he'd let her go without a word of apology for scaring her or misreading how she'd receive taking their relationship another step.

That's why he'd called her just now, to try to smooth over what had been a misstep. He'd never imagined she'd push him away the way she had.

"You look like you literally could bite a steel bar in two," Andrew said as he leaned in the open doorway to Roman's office.

"I'm fine. Just didn't sleep well."

"You are the smartest person I've ever met, but you are a pitiful liar. It's the whole nice guy thing you have going on. Lying makes your face contort strangely."

Roman shot his best friend an eat-crap-and-die look.

With each passing moment, Anna's words ate a bit deeper into him. Though it felt like something was off, he still couldn't help being...well, angry. Not that he'd ever expect a woman to go out with him simply because he wanted her to. That kind of attitude would have his mother reaching down from Heaven to shake some respect into him.

"Lady troubles?" Andrew asked.

"You could say that."

"Don't tell me all those McQueen good looks and charm have failed you."

"Evidently they don't count for much."

Andrew's teasing expression slid off his face. "What happened?"

Roman wasn't thrilled with the idea of spilling everything, but maybe Andrew could give him an outside perspective and help him figure out what the heck was going on. After he'd finished telling him about all the events leading up to his dinner with Anna the night before, the kiss, her reaction to it and then their phone conversation, Andrew ran his hand back through his hair.

"Women, huh?"

Roman sighed. "You're no help at all."

"Sorry, man. Trying to lighten the mood, which didn't work. Listen, I agree with you. Something doesn't add up. Whether that's Anna being fickle or scared or you really did just read her interest wrong, I don't know. You know her better than I do."

"I thought I did."

"Let her sit with her decision for a while. Go out with someone else to get your mind off everything. Maybe Anna will change her mind and let you know."

Though they had gotten to a point where they could talk more easily, he couldn't imagine someone as naturally introverted as Anna taking that step even if she wanted to. Which left him in one really crappy situation.

He somehow made it through his two-hour shift at the free clinic after work. For a while, he was even able to forget his troubles as he listened to those with real trials in their lives.

When he pulled into his driveway, he noticed Kailee a couple of houses down struggling with a toppled mailbox.

"Did you drive over it?" he asked as he walked in her direction.

"No, someone else did, and I bet I know who it was. Paul, the package delivery guy. He drives down this street like it's the freaking Autobahn or something."

"Here, let me help you with that." He righted the pole and poured in the quick-setting concrete she had at the ready. "How's the planning for the block party going?"

"Not so hot. Everyone has such different schedules between work and their kids' activities. I just really wanted to do something fun besides parking in front of my TV and binge watching stuff. At the rate I'm going, I'm going to weigh a ton before winter."

He laughed at the very thought. "I cannot see that happening." It hit him that he'd just laughed on a day when he'd not felt the least bit like laughing. "We should go do something soon." He worried he'd just stepped in it by the way her eyes widened in obvious excitement.

"I'd like that. Say, are you off work Saturday? My cousin has a little art exhibit opening in Gardiner. Would you be interested in going to that?"

"Sure. It's been a while since I've been down that far anyway. Maybe we could visit the park, too."

"Awesome. I can walk off some of my TV snacks."

Any normal guy his age would be thrilled at the idea of spending a day with a woman as friendly and outgoing and beautiful as Kailee, but as Roman stepped into his house several minutes later and sank onto his couch all he could think about was a shy librarian who liked chocolate milkshakes.

ANNA WAS PRETTY sure her heart was broken, but she had no one to blame but herself. Paige had told her she was a fool for what she'd done, and a very large part of Anna thought she was right. Several times she'd even picked up her phone with the aim of calling Roman, apologizing, telling him how she really felt, but she always stopped short of dialing his number. How could she know she was being irrational and still not be able to excavate the doubts that plagued her, the ones created by years of hearing her grandmother preach them like the gospel and her own lackluster dating history?

Feeling the walls of her house closing in on her, she decided to get outside and try to enjoy some time in nature, clear her mind. She drove south out of Logan Springs toward Yellowstone National Park. She'd found peace there before when life was stressful, so she hoped it would work its magic again.

After driving through the gateway community of Gardiner, she entered the park through the stone Roosevelt Arch, reading the words inscribed on it as she passed underneath: For the Benefit and Enjoyment of the People. She noticed tourists pulled off to the side of the road taking photos of a group of elk. They had much more impressive views of wildlife ahead of them once they drove deeper into the park.

Since when most tourists reached the headquarters area at Mammoth Hot Springs they tended to continue south toward the geyser basin and Old Faithful, Anna took a left and headed across the northern section of the park. It was the kind of gorgeous day in a comparatively wild place that tended to make the real world and a person's cares seem far away. And while she wasn't immune to the beauty surrounding her, Anna's cares were riding shotgun.

She needed to get out and move, so she pulled over near the Wraith Falls trailhead. She liked visiting the parts of the park that didn't draw the larger crowds because the peacefulness felt more real at the overlooked gems. The wildflowers were putting on quite a show as she headed out across the meadow. She bet this would be something Roman would like, too.

No, she had to stop thinking about him. That's what this day was about. But it proved impossible to keep thoughts of him or that kiss they'd shared from invading her mind. Even spotting a ground squirrel or a family of deer didn't deter her thoughts for more than a few seconds.

She tried focusing on other aspects of her life as she crossed over Lupine Creek and made the turn that preceded the climb up to the viewing platform near the base of the falls. She'd used the money from the trail ride to buy the car, so she'd dipped into her savings to start paying the medical bills. And despite what Roman had said about her trying writing mysteries again, she couldn't face being rejected right now. Instead, she'd sent out queries to a few librarian publications with some article ideas. Hopefully, those would pan out, but if they didn't it wouldn't feel the same as a rejection of something she'd created out of her own imagination.

She reached the viewing platform and stared up at the simple beauty of Wraith Falls, so named because of their shape, which reminded early visitors of a ghost. Anna didn't sense any spirits, just the gentle breeze in the surrounding Douglas firs and the flow of the water over the ridged, flat rock face. She closed her eyes and breathed deeply, slowly in and out. The sound of small animals scurrying in and around the fallen fir trees actually made her smile.

She'd been right to come here. No, her heartache about Roman wasn't gone, but she could breathe more easily here than pacing around her house where she'd spent a weekend binge watching TV with him.

After a while, she heard the sound of voices and glanced down the trail to see a young couple laughing and joking with each other as they climbed to where she stood. She'd leave in a moment, but she turned her gaze back to the falls for a final look.

"Oh, hi," the young woman said when she saw Anna. "We thought we were the only people out here."

"I was just leaving."

"You don't have to go."

Anna smiled. "I've been out here a while. Lots more to see."

"Before you go, could you take our picture?"

"Sure." She accepted the petite blonde's phone and took a few photos of the lovebirds with the falls in the background. They looked so happy and in love, and for a moment Anna pictured herself and Roman in their spot.

"Thanks so much."

"No problem. Enjoy your visit." Anna made her way back down the switchbacks in the trail, out of range of hearing the couple, then took her time back across the meadow. When she finally returned to her car, she made her way to the Lamar Valley and took several photos of a large bison herd that had drawn a crowd of people, some also with their phones out and others with the types of huge, costly lenses that signaled they were serious photographers.

She gradually made her way back to Mammoth Hot Springs. By the time she got there, she was so thirsty she stopped at the park store to grab some water and a snack. While inside, she perused all the cool park-themed offerings but made her way toward the cash register with only her water and a bag of trail mix. But next to a display of Yellowstone T-shirts, she stopped in her tracks the moment her gaze met Roman's.

Of all the places he could be right now, it had to be here. All the effort she'd put into not thinking about him disappeared in an instant.

And then she saw he wasn't alone. Kailee, the woman she'd met at the restaurant the night Roman had kissed her, stepped up next to him with a smile so bright she could be in a toothpaste commercial.

Though it felt as if she was trying to lift the entire Absaroka Range, Anna managed to force a smile of her own. After all, she was the one who'd ended things with Roman before they could really get started.

"I see I wasn't the only one with the idea to get out and enjoy the day," she said.

"Oh, hey," Kailee said. "Anna, right?"

"Yeah." Anna wasn't the type to hate others, but she had to admit there was a little part of her that wanted to hate Kailee. But that wasn't fair because the other woman hadn't done a single thing wrong. Neither had Roman. The fault for this awkward, tense situation lay entirely at Anna's feet.

Her gaze shifted to Roman, who hadn't said a word. He looked like he wanted to but didn't know what to say.

"How are you?" he finally asked, likely more out of courtesy than any real desire to know.

"Fine. You?"

And the award for the most awkward, useless conversation goes to...

"Okay." He seemed to remember he was with someone and glanced over at Kailee. "Kailee's cousin is having a gallery showing in Gardiner tonight, so we came up here for a bit before that."

"That sounds nice." Her words threatened to choke her.

"You should come," Kailee said. "Avery is a talented painter. I'm envious, really. My artistic talent extends only to those turkeys we drew in elementary school by running the pencil around our fingers and thumb."

The idea of being around Roman while he was with another woman was at the absolute bottom of Anna's list of fun things to do. As in she wasn't going to that gallery show in a million years.

"Thank you for the invitation, but I have plans tonight." Plans to call herself a fool over and over. "I hope you have a nice time."

With a nod goodbye, Anna resisted the urge to just toss her water and trail mix on the nearest shelf and make a run for it. Instead, she acted as if the sight of Roman with another woman hadn't bothered her and made her way to the cash register. Miraculously, she didn't cry, though she felt the burning need to. Because if she started, she was afraid she wouldn't stop.

★

HE COULDN'T LOOK at her. No matter how much he wanted to go after Anna and ask her face to face why she'd pushed him away, the real reason, he didn't. He had always taken women at their word, respected their decisions. And besides, it would be rude and inconsiderate to Kailee.

Still, as he and Kailee stepped outside he couldn't get the look he'd seen on Anna's face out of his head. When they'd first made eye contact across the store, she'd looked as shocked as he felt. And he'd swear he saw pain, which in a strange way gave him hope. If she didn't have feelings for him, she wouldn't care who he took out.

"She's more than a friend, isn't she?"

The sound of Kailee's voice pulled him out of his own head. When he looked her way, he saw from her sad smile that she could see the truth of how he felt. It would be wrong to lie to her.

"We're not together."

"But you want to be."

He sighed as he looked out over the lawn area where a herd of elk were lazing away while tourists took pictures of them.

"I do, but she doesn't."

"I don't think that's true."

He looked over at her. "What makes you say that?"

"I'm a woman. She's a woman. I know pining when I see

it."

So he hadn't imagined it?

"I'm sorry."

She waved off his apology. "Don't worry about it. Will I mourn an opportunity with my hot doctor neighbor? Sure. But I'll live. I'm a firm believer in people being with someone who makes them happy and who they can make happy in return."

A sense of shame came over Roman. He'd misjudged Kailee. There was a lot more to her than a casual, quick conversation indicated.

"You're a kind person," he said. "I hope you find someone who sweeps you off your feet and is really good to you."

"Me, too. But don't think this is getting you out of going to the gallery show."

He laughed a little. "I wouldn't dream of it."

They got into his truck and headed back down toward Gardiner, him wondering if there was anything he could do to change the situation with Anna for the better.

"You should tell her how you feel," Kailee said suddenly.

"Am I that obvious?"

"Yep, but that's okay. And I'm serious. Even if something is keeping Anna from admitting how she really feels, you should tell her."

"I don't want to push her after she said she wasn't interested."

"You don't have to push. Just make a full confession and then leave the next move up to her. I'm assuming you haven't actually told her how you feel, right?"

"I don't suppose kissing her counts?"

She gave him a look that telegraphed the thought that men really were dim, no matter how many advanced degrees they had.

"Um, no. Use your words."

He smiled at her. "Yes, ma'am."

In between making small talk with Kailee, her cousin and other people at the art show, Roman tried to determine exactly which words to use when he saw Anna again. It felt as if his entire future depended on picking the right ones.

CHAPTER FIFTEEN

A S ANNA PULLED into her driveway, she didn't think she could muster the energy to go inside. She hadn't felt this drained since she was in the hospital. When she looked through the windshield, her mood shifted unexpectedly. A sudden wave of anger pushed the sadness to the side, but it wasn't anger with herself this time. The target was her grandmother, for how she'd done her damnedest to indoctrinate Anna so fully to her point of view that Anna hadn't trusted her own feelings or judgment.

She started the car again and drove out of Logan Springs toward Livingston. Chances were more than even that her grandmother wouldn't even know her, but Anna had some things to say nonetheless. A voice, a knowledge deep inside told her that the only way she was going to be able to fully and finally break free of her grandmother's beliefs and forge her own was to face the woman who'd cost her so much—self-confidence, a belief she could aspire to bigger dreams, any real family. Even Roman. Because after how she'd treated him, she had a hard time imagining him giving her a second chance. Besides, he'd already moved on, so that kiss must not have meant as much to him as it had her.

Stop it! That's Helena talking.

By the time she reached the nursing home, she was shaking. She took a few minutes to calm down as much as she could before going inside. The attendant at the front desk was on the phone but recognized Anna and buzzed her in. Anna's feet felt as if she was walking through wet concrete as she approached her grandmother's room. She'd second-guessed coming here. What good would it do? It wasn't as if she could even have an actual argument with Helena. Despite everything, she suddenly realized how cruel it would be to confront a woman who didn't even remember doing the things that had so upset Anna.

But she was already here, and she hadn't seen her grandmother since before her wreck. No matter what had happened, Anna felt enough duty toward the woman who'd raised her that she visited Helena even though it was almost always a one-sided conversation.

After taking another fortifying breath, she pushed open the door and found Helena lying in bed watching TV. Anna didn't know if what was happening on the screen even registered in Helena's brain.

The fatigue she'd felt before the burst of anger had fueled her drive here swamped her, and she dropped into a recliner next to the bed. Helena didn't even acknowledge her presence.

It was all just too much. The tears broke free, flowing down her cheeks as sobs took over. A lifetime of heartache spilled out. A father who didn't want her. A mother who left her behind as if she meant nothing. A grandmother too cynical to believe in hope or aspiration. Her own mistakes.

"Why did you make me this way?" she asked, the words raw as they escaped between sobs. "Why couldn't you allow me to dream? To believe I could grab true happiness instead of doubting the motives of everyone around me?"

Helena didn't have any answers. She never would.

Anna didn't know how long she sat there with her unresponsive grandmother, crying her eyes out. By the time she finally expunged all her tears, she had a raging headache, itchy eyes and a stuffy nose. So that she didn't look as if she'd come from the room of someone who'd just died she washed her face in the small bathroom. She paused next to her grandmother and wondered what her life might be like now if Helena had been the loving, sweet, doting type of grandparent. Like so many other things, she'd never know.

She reached out and straightened the sweater that had slipped off Helena's shoulder. "I'm sorry you weren't able to find happiness in your life. And I'm really sorry you ended up here, like this."

She wasn't totally without affection for Helena. There were even some good memories if she thought about it. They were just too often eclipsed by the not so great and Helena's jaded outlook on life. How miserable it must have been to live one's entire adult life that way.

Well, Anna wasn't about to follow in her grandmother's or her mother's footsteps. As soon as she stepped out of this room, she was going to figure out how to forge a path that was uniquely her own.

⭐

ANNA WAS SO lost in her thoughts as she drove down her street that she didn't immediately see the large SUV sitting in front of her house. She lifted her foot from the accelerator and considered circling the block, hoping the vehicle would be gone when she got back. As she drew close, she noticed the license plate was from Colorado and the man sitting inside was looking at his phone. Maybe he was a tourist who had somehow managed to get lost. That would take some doing considering Highway 89 was a straight shot from the interstate to the park and ending up on her street would have required turning off the main road.

She was so tired she was seeing potential threats where there weren't any. Instead of giving in to that paranoia, she pulled into her driveway. But when she got out of the car, she noticed the man had stepped from his as well. She eyed the house, knowing she couldn't unlock the door and get safely inside before he overtook her if he was here for some nefarious purpose. Instead, she stayed next to her open car door.

"Anna?"

Her concern ratcheted up. How did he know her name? She didn't give him an answer either way.

"I'm sorry to just show up like this, but I wanted to meet you in person."

She scoured her brain, trying to figure out who this man might be. Was he a bill collector? If so, bill collecting paid pretty well. But she wasn't to that stage with her medical bills yet.

Holding up a hand, she said, "Stay right there."

He stopped moving forward and extended his own hands in an "I mean no harm" gesture.

"I didn't intend to scare you."

"Who are you?"

He hesitated a moment and then smiled. "I'm your father."

Anna stared at him, wondering if she'd cracked. Was he a hallucination? But he was still there after she blinked. This day had to be the wildest emotional roller coaster ride of her life—even more than waking up in a coma.

ANNA NEEDED SLEEP almost more than she needed air to breathe. She wished she could hit pause and get a good night's rest before she had to face this man who claimed to be her father. How many times had she wanted to know who he was? Why he'd not wanted her? Now the answers were quite possibly across the small bakery buying her coffee, and she was so spent she could barely think straight.

She'd told the man, who said his name was Randall Stevens, to meet her here. No way was she going to let a stranger into her home, no matter who he claimed he was.

"Here you go," he said as he slid a coffee and a cherry Danish in front of her.

She wasn't in the mood to eat, but she took a giant gulp of the coffee. Hopefully the caffeine would kick in quickly.

"I'm sure you have lots of questions," he said as he sat across from her.

"Why didn't you want me?"

"Right to the point."

"It's kind of the most pressing question. I've been waiting to ask it for a long time."

"I didn't know at first."

"But you found out at some later point."

"Yes."

He wasn't exactly flooding her with information.

"When?"

"Your mother was about six months pregnant."

"And you told her what when you found out?"

He took a breath and fiddled with his coffee cup. "I was a married man, already had two kids." He said it as if that explained away his decision to ignore his third child.

"Your wife didn't know about my mother, did she?"

He had the decency to look embarrassed. "No."

She took another drink of coffee and then managed a bite of her Danish when her stomach growled from lack of food.

"I'm sorry your mother didn't raise you."

"She was a broken woman, always looking for something she couldn't have." That old fear that despite her best efforts she might end up the same way tried to claw its way back into her mind, but she mentally slapped it away.

"Tell me about your life," he said.

Did she want to share details with this man who had waited three decades to deign to be a part of her life? She considered walking away, but then she remembered that as she slowly lost her grandmother Randall would be the only blood relative she'd have left. She thought back on all the times she'd wanted so desperately to know the identity of her father.

And so she began to tell him the life story of Anna Mae Kenner.

She felt as if she was reciting her autobiography. He responded in kind but admittedly with fewer details. Dinah McQueen, who owned the bakery, came by to refill their coffees and gave Anna a curious look. Anna managed a small smile to let the other woman know she was okay.

"So why search for me after all these years?"

"I should have done it years ago. I'm not proud that I didn't."

"But you didn't." Suspicion started to twist inside her. Something was off.

He clasped his hands on the table and took a deep breath. "Yes, there's another reason for me being here now, and it's going to sound like a selfish one. No, it *is* a selfish one." He paused, took a breath. "I have cancer, and we've so far been unsuccessful finding a bone marrow donor."

Anna would swear he'd punched her in the stomach.

Had this entire evening been a performance, a way to soften her up and make her believe her father suddenly wanted to be a part of her life in case she might be able to save him?

It was all suddenly too much. This day had frayed every single one of her nerves, and she had to get out of here. She nearly knocked her chair over in her haste to get away from this man, this stranger who had contributed nothing more to her life than some DNA.

Randall started to stand, too. "Anna?"

She held out a hand to stop him. "No, don't. I can't handle this right now."

Before she could have a nervous breakdown in the middle of the bakery, she hurried toward the exit. It was possible she looked wild-eyed crazy as she nearly ran toward her car, but at the moment she didn't care. She needed to be alone, away from every single person on the planet. If she was alone, no one could hurt her.

Roman wanted to go to sleep, then wake up in the morning with the answers to what he should do about Anna. Based on what Kailee had said, he didn't think he had imagined how Anna was affected by seeing him with Kailee. But did that mean she regretted nixing any sort of romantic relationship between them? He didn't want to push, but his gut was telling him that all was not as it seemed on the surface.

He leaned his head against the back of his couch. His eyes had just drifted closed when his phone rang, startling him out of his meandering thoughts. His heart rate picked up at the thought that maybe it was Anna calling, that she was taking the initiative and he wouldn't have to figure out the right step, if any, to take himself. But it was Dinah's number on the phone display.

Maybe talking to his cousin would take his mind off things for a few minutes.

"Hey," he said in answer.

"Hey, yourself. Where are you now?"

"Um, home. Where should I be?" Had he somehow forgotten some sort of family gathering?

"Nowhere. I mean…listen, I just witnessed something and I'm not sure I should tell you because I don't know where you and Anna stand right now."

"Current status could be described as acquaintances." No reason to tell her about running into Anna in the park and the look he'd seen on her face. "But what's going on? Is something wrong?"

"Anna came into the bakery earlier with an older guy, like mid-fifties or early sixties maybe. I'm terrible at guessing ages. They sat and talked for quite a while, and Anna just had this look about her—like she had these invisible walls up around her or something. And then he must have said something that upset her because she stood up suddenly and then left in a hurry."

Roman was already on his feet, pacing. "Did he follow

her?"

"No. It looked like she told him to stay, and he did. But Roman, the look on her face when she left. It was as if she'd been shattered. I couldn't go after her myself, and I didn't know who else to call. I tried Paige, but I didn't get an answer."

"It's fine. I'll check on her."

But when he hung up and dialed Anna's number, he was already out the front door and running to his truck. When she didn't answer, he left her a message that he was on his way, to call him because he was worried about her, that Dinah had called him concerned about her. He tried not to panic as he broke the speed limit by a considerable margin as he drove toward Logan Springs.

EVERY TIME SHE didn't think she had any tears left, Anna proved herself wrong. She lay curled up in the middle of her bed wishing she could magically transport herself to the other side of the world, to an entirely different life. Just as she'd made the decision to break free of her grandmother's thinking, her father walked back into her life and gave her hope that maybe she could have family again. But he only cared about what she could give him after a lifetime of him not giving her anything, not even acknowledgment of her existence.

Though she didn't feel like moving, the need to go to the

bathroom forced her to. When she was done and caught sight of herself in the mirror, she looked dreadful. Red, swollen eyes. Splotchy skin. Messy hair. And her head pounded as if there were tiny men inside her head hammering on her skull.

She turned on the water and washed her hands and then her face. As she was drying off, she heard her phone ringing from where she'd left it on the kitchen table. She wasn't in the mood to talk to anyone, least of all the man who claimed to be her father, so she ignored it.

But as she left the bathroom, someone started knocking on the front door. She froze. Was Randall a violent man? Would he try to force her to give him what he wanted? She eased down the hallway and into the living room so she could peek out the window. But it wasn't Randall at the door. No, it was her first heartbreak of the day.

She sighed as she walked to the door, wishing she didn't look like complete crap.

When she opened the door, he had his hand up ready to knock again. For a couple of seconds, they just stared at each other.

"Thank God you're all right," he said.

Did he think she would hurt herself after seeing him with Kailee? Then it hit her.

"Dinah told you what happened at the bakery."

"What she could see."

Since he didn't look like he was going to leave and she didn't want to invite in mosquitoes, she stepped back and gestured for Roman to come inside.

"You've been crying," he said.

"You're really observant." She wasn't normally sarcastic, but she'd had one hell of a day.

Roman stepped forward and placed his hands lightly on her shoulders. The contact, combined with her frayed emotions, made her lower lip tremble.

"Tell me what happened." It wasn't a command, but rather an offer of a willing ear and potential comfort. Despite how she'd pushed him away, he was still there for her.

She'd only thought she didn't have more tears to shed. The moment a sob escaped her again, Roman pulled her into his arms and held her close, rubbing her back. And she brokenly told him about her father showing up on her doorstep and her foolishly getting her hopes up only to have them dashed.

Somewhere in the middle of her recounting, Roman steered them to the couch. Though she didn't tell him, the memory of that weekend they'd spent there together, watching TV, stuffing their faces and laughing, contributed to some of her tears.

She should pull away from him, but she just couldn't make herself do it. He felt too good, and she needed to not feel so alone. She'd give herself a little while longer to soak up his warmth and comforting embrace before she pulled herself back to reality. This felt so nice, and it tempted her to believe they could have a future... But she'd seen him with someone else.

She scooted away from him. "I'm sorry. Kailee wouldn't like this."

Roman captured her hand. "Kailee and I are friends, nothing more."

She sensed he was about to say something else, something she didn't currently have the willpower to resist, so she stood and took a couple of steps away.

"Thank you for coming by. You didn't have to."

Roman stood. "Anna."

She shook her head. "I'm really tired. All I want to do right now is go to sleep."

Roman sighed and looked away for a moment, as if to rein in what he wanted to say, before meeting her gaze again.

"Call me if you need anything, okay? Even to talk."

She nodded, more to get him and the temptation he presented to leave than any intent to take him up on his offer. When he closed the distance between them, she didn't have time to react before he dropped a quick kiss on her forehead then headed out the front door.

As she listened to him walk to his truck, get in, shut the door, start the engine, back out of the driveway and head down the street, she didn't move. It was as if her body had forgotten how, leaving her standing in the middle of her living room wondering if she would ever be able to take a step again. And if she was, what it would be.

CHAPTER SIXTEEN

B<small>EFORE LEAVING</small> L<small>OGAN</small> Springs, Roman stopped to get gas. He wanted to find the man claiming to be Anna's father and punish him for breaking Anna's heart, for being one more person in her life to let her down.

As he was returning the nozzle to the pump, he saw Parker Varton pull up in his sheriff's department vehicle. Before he went against his oath and did some harm, he walked over to speak to Parker.

"Hey, you got a minute?"

"Sure. Can I get a coffee first? I'm on duty all night."

Roman nodded then leaned against the warm hood of Parker's SUV and waited until he returned with a large coffee and a package of mini chocolate doughnuts.

Roman lifted a brow. "Doughnuts, really?"

"Bite me. I've liked these since I was a kid."

"They're bad for you."

"So I've heard. Now what did you want to talk about?"

He told Parker what had transpired at the bakery and how upset Anna was about the ordeal.

"Can you see if this guy is who he says he is?"

"Yeah."

When Roman got back in his truck, the reality of how tired he was slammed into him. He wanted nothing more than to turn around and go back to Anna's, to curl up next to her. The idea of driving home and crawling into his bed by himself seemed mighty damn lonely tonight.

ROMAN LEFT THE hospital after his final rounds the next day to find Paige sitting on the bench outside the ER.

"Paige? Is something wrong?" He glanced back at the ER. "Anna?"

"She's fine. Well, not fine, but then you know that already." She patted the bench seat next to her. "I'm actually here to see you."

Now that he knew Anna wasn't a patient in the ER again, he lowered himself to the bench.

"I'm probably overstepping the bounds of friendship here, but I'm going to do it anyway because I love Anna and I want her to be happy. I think you could make her happy if she'd just get out of her own way."

"So I'm not crazy in believing she's hiding something?"

"I don't know if I'd call it hiding. That sounds too nefarious or something. She's just not being totally honest, and it's not entirely her fault."

He knew he must look confused because Paige turned toward him and held up her index finger as if to say, "Wait, I'm going to explain."

"Her entire life, the only family that has consistently been there is her grandmother, but while Helena took care of all of Anna's physical needs the same can't be said of the emotional ones. Helena's life didn't end up how she wanted, and neither did her daughter's, so she just got more bitter by the year. And she firmly believed that the key to making it through life was not to aspire too high, whether that had to do with jobs, expectations of other people, or falling in love. She shoved that thought—that people should only pair up with people of their own social standing—into Anna's head from as far back as she can remember, so much that while Anna might not have accepted it as absolute truth, she's always doubted her judgment of other people. So when she started falling for you, she kept thinking about how it was probably safer to deny her feelings because it would likely never work out."

Roman gestured for Paige to pause. "Wait, that doesn't make any sense. Anna and I are from the same place, both college-educated; we're not that different."

"Oh, it's sweet that you think that. It makes me like you even more. But let's think about this for a moment. You're not only a doctor and from one of the wealthiest families in Montana, but you also grew up in the midst of a loving family. How does that resemble Anna's life at all?"

It hit him just how much he took all the positive aspects of his life for granted, even after everything he'd been through. The fact that Paige had said Anna was falling for him also settled front and center in his mind.

"Did she say she was…falling for me?"

Paige grinned. "She didn't have to. I know that girl better than she knows herself. Half of what I just told you she's never told me. I figured it out."

"What do I do? I don't want to push her or make her feel uncomfortable."

"Just tell her how you really feel and don't give up on her. She's fighting against a lifetime of learning what Helena preached, which is equivalent to some sort of caste system. 'Don't marry, don't date, don't even like someone above your station. It only leads to heartbreak.'"

He clenched the edge of the bench. "I don't like to think ill of someone in Helena's state, but I'm more than a little angry with her right now."

"Welcome to the club. That woman did a number on our girl."

He looked over at Paige. "What made you think I feel the same way about Anna that you say she feels about me?"

"I have eyes and ears. And no one works that hard and goes that far out of his way to help someone without being in love with her."

In love with her? Did his feelings run that deep?

Yes. Somewhere between reading to her while she was in that coma and now, he'd fallen for Anna Kenner. Now he just had to find a way to convince her that he'd never hurt her, no matter how much money his family had.

★

"YOU OKAY, DR. McQueen?"

Roman met the gaze of his last patient of the day, Minnie Forstell, the embodiment of a sweet little grandmother.

"Yes. I think I'm the one supposed to be asking you that."

She waved off his concern. "I'm completely fine. I wouldn't even be here if I wasn't required to come in once a year to get my asthma prescription refilled. But you look like there's something weighing heavy on your mind."

"Just another man trying to figure out the complexities of relationships."

"Oh, who's the lucky lady?"

He waggled his finger at her. "Nope. There will be no wheedling it out of me."

She pouted. "Well, you're no fun. A lady my age has to live vicariously, you know?"

He smiled. "I'll make you a deal. If it works out, I'll let you know the next time I see you."

"You better."

As soon as Minnie left, he turned to finish up his notes on their visit. When he was done and shut the laptop before securing it in a locked cabinet, he picked up his cell phone and called Parker to see if he'd found out anything yet.

"Funny you should pick right now to call," Parker said when he answered.

"How's that? Did you find out something?"

"Dude checks out. He owns a big construction company in Denver, like I'm talking they build sports stadiums level construction."

So the guy was that well-off and hadn't seen fit to give his daughter one red cent. But he could sure show up on her doorstep when he needed something. Roman barely held in a curse.

"But the more interesting part is that he either is trying to buy his way into Anna's good graces or, rather, hopefully feels like the giant heel he is because he just left after offering a sizeable reward for information leading to the arrest of the person who ran Anna off the road."

If literally any other person had offered up that cash, he'd be grateful without reservations. As it was, the news left him conflicted because he suspected an ulterior motive. Plus, he was annoyed he hadn't thought of doing it himself. But he also realized that might have been a step too far considering his and Anna's relationship.

"Roman, you there?"

"Yeah. Think it'll do any good?"

"Some people will turn in their own mom for a reward, so if it's someone from around here I wouldn't be surprised."

At least that would be a good result, no matter the motive.

After the call ended, he considered calling to check up on Anna and tell her what he'd just learned. But now that he wasn't acting in the heat of the moment, he acknowledged that it hadn't been his place to do a background check on her father. He'd just wanted so much to protect her from any further harm.

But he still wanted to see her. He'd thought a lot about what Paige had told him, considered a lot of different ways to tell Anna his feelings so she'd believe him. He still didn't know if any of the ideas would work, but he wouldn't know until he tried. And so he hung up his lab coat, put away his stethoscope and headed toward Logan Springs.

ANNA POINTED TOWARD the computer screen in front of Mary Wayborn. "If you click here, it'll take you to the 1820 census records."

"Wow, who knew all this information was out there? This is so exciting, finding out about relatives that long ago."

Anna smiled and moved on to the next station. Since she and Paige had come up with the idea for monthly genealogy nights at the library six months ago, the event had drawn more people each month. But tonight the last thing she felt like discussing was family ties. Luckily, all she had to do was typically point her patrons in the right direction. Paige was busy helping a couple of people check out books since they kept the regular library services open during special event nights.

The front door opened, revealing the last person she'd expected to see tonight.

"Hey," she said. "I thought you had your family traced back to before Montana even became a state."

"Huh?"

At his confused look, she motioned to all the people sitting at computers. "Genealogy night."

"Oh, I'm not here for that. I need to check out some research books."

Now it was her turn to be confused. "You know there's a library in Livingston, right?"

"Yes, but I know the librarian here."

She caught a few of the patrons at the computers looking their direction, so she motioned him toward the circulation desk.

"What kind of research books are you looking for?"

"Something that will teach me how to win a woman's heart."

Anna almost tripped over her own feet.

"You see," Roman continued, "there's this woman that I really like a lot and I think she might like me, too, but she's...I guess you could call it skittish. And I want to find a way to assure her that I'll never do anything to hurt her. That she can trust me with her heart if she feels the same way about me."

Anna's heart was currently busy trying to test the limits of the human heart rate.

"Roman," she said under her breath.

"I know it's hard for you to trust people, and I understand why. But I can't go another day without saying in plain words how I feel. I'm falling for you, Anna Kenner, and I really hope you feel the same."

She shook her head.

"Stop," he said. "I can almost hear all the reasons why we can't work that you're manufacturing in that brain of yours, and they're all wrong. This is not just a passing thing. I tried to go out with someone else. It didn't work. Even Kailee could tell how I feel about you, and she also said she could tell that those feelings weren't just going one direction." He paused, and she was pretty certain everyone in the building could hear the pounding of her heart. Roman stepped closer to her and took her fingers in his. "Was she wrong?"

Anna couldn't deny it anymore. Not to herself. Not to Roman.

"No."

His fingers entwined with hers, and when she looked up he was smiling so wide she felt as if she were standing in the first warm sun of spring after a long, cold winter.

"You think Paige could handle the rest of genealogy night?"

"Yes. Yes, she can," Paige called out, eliciting laughs from the people who'd abandoned their searches for long-lost ancestors.

"I guess there's your answer." Anna felt like giggling as she went to retrieve her purse. She wondered just how red her face was when she accompanied Roman through the front door into the twilight outside.

As soon as they rounded the corner to the parking lot,

Roman spun her into his arms, eliciting a little surprised yelp from her. And then he was kissing her like she was the only woman in the world.

✪

STRANGE. THAT'S HOW it felt to believe she could have a future, one well beyond anything she'd allowed herself to imagine.

After they'd left the library, Roman had driven them to a pretty spot beside the river and then produced an actual picnic basket filled with a meal from the Pinnacle, the restaurant at his family's resort. They'd sat on a blanket and eaten as the last of the day's light faded over the mountains. Then they'd lain side by side staring up at the stars talking about big things—what she was going to do about her father—as well as the inconsequential. And they'd kissed. A lot.

She could still feel the soft warmth of his lips moving against hers even though he was probably back in Livingston by now. She'd almost thrown all caution out the window and invited him to stay the night, but she needed time to process what had happened. The fact that she had decided to give a relationship with Roman a chance. To stave off the lingering fear that it could be a mistake.

No, stop thinking like that. You're done being that person.

She had just crawled into bed when her phone dinged with a text. When she saw the words on the screen from

Roman, she was surprised her smile didn't light up the room.

Good night, beautiful.

For a few moments, she held the phone against her heart, not quite believing the turn her life had taken after some terrible lows.

✪

ANNA JERKED AWAKE with her heart slamming against her rib cage. For several panicked moments, the grief consumed her. But gradually she realized what she'd just experienced was only a nightmare. A truly heartbreaking nightmare.

When she felt she could stand, she went to the bathroom and washed her face with cold water. She still felt shaky when she returned to sit on the side of her bed.

The dream had been so real, one of those that lingered because it ripped such raw emotion from you when you were defenseless against it. The kind that made you question whether it was dream or premonition.

But no, Roman's cancer had not returned. And it hadn't killed him. He had regular checkups, and as a doctor he knew signs that should cause concern. This was likely just her subconscious worried about allowing herself to get involved with him.

To love him.

Because she did. If that dream proved anything, it was

that she'd fallen totally in love with Roman and that losing him was the absolute worst pain she could imagine.

But maybe the dream meant something else entirely. She considered how awful she felt thinking of losing Roman and realized that her father's wife would likely feel the same if she lost him. If Anna could prevent that, she had to. It didn't matter that her father hadn't been a father at all to her. He was still a human being facing a scary diagnosis.

Still feeling jittery, she grabbed her phone and called the resort where he was staying. The way their first meeting had ended hadn't led to the exchange of cell numbers. She didn't even know if he'd stuck around. He could very well be back in Colorado thinking he might die.

But the person who answered the phone connected her to his room. He sounded both surprised and relieved to hear from her.

"I'm going to the hospital to get tested."

"Would you like me to go with you?"

"No." She still wasn't ready to face him yet. "I'll let you know the results as soon as I have them."

"Thank you. And Anna…I'm so sorry, for everything."

"Thank you for saying that."

She ended the call and set about figuring out what she needed to do to see if she was a match for her father, a sense of the surreal accompanying her every step.

★

ANNA HAD TO give Roman credit. While she awaited the results of her tests, he did his best to distract her. Not that it was particularly hard because a single kiss from him sent her mind spinning into a bright, dizzying bliss.

They went on dates like a normal couple, had dinner with his family on more than one occasion, and texted each other throughout the days when they were at their respective jobs. She felt as if she walked around with a perpetual grin on her face. One day at the library, Paige pulled her into a hug for no reason.

"What was that for?"

"I'm just so happy to see you happy."

And before her father had to go back to Colorado, she even spent more time with him. All was not forgiven, but she had hope that they'd at least have a relationship from now on. He'd also surprised her with a hug before he left. The even bigger surprise was how much she'd held on to him, needing some sort of connection to family.

Though she also felt as if she was being welcomed into the McQueen family. They were kind, loving, funny—everything she'd ever dreamed about having. But a tiny part of her still worried that in the end things might not work out. Granted, that voice was smaller than it used to be, but it was still there. She wondered if it might always linger.

As she walked down the sidewalk in Livingston to meet Roman at the restaurant where they'd eaten the night of their first kiss, her phone rang. Thinking it might be him she paused on the sidewalk and answered.

Instead it was Parker Varton.

"Hi, Parker."

"I have some news I thought you might like to hear. We just arrested the guy who ran you off the road. He admitted to being intoxicated at the time."

"How did you find him after all this time?"

"The reward money."

"What reward?"

Parker hesitated, as if perhaps he'd revealed something he shouldn't have. "Your dad put up a reward for information leading to the arrest."

"He did?"

"Yeah."

He'd done that without telling her, so there had been no ulterior motive. She warmed a bit more toward him, but she was still feeling stunned when she reached the restaurant.

"What's wrong?" Roman asked as soon as he saw her.

"Nothing." She looked at the phone still in her hand. "I just got a call from Parker. They've arrested the guy who caused my accident."

He took her hands in his. "How about we go to my place and order pizza instead?"

"I'd like that." She hadn't realized she suddenly wasn't in the mood for sitting out in public, but Roman had seen it and offered her a way out. Yet another reason to love him. She almost told him standing right there at the entrance to the restaurant, but that didn't seem like the right setting or the right time. Plus, she thought he felt the same, but he'd never actually said the words.

Would she never be totally free of the doubt that seemed to be woven into her very DNA?

When they were settled at his house, a hot, cheesy pizza newly delivered, Roman looked across the table at her.

"Can I confess something?"

Dread filled her. Was he already having second thoughts about being with her?

"Uh, sure."

"I knew about the reward your dad offered."

That had not been what she was expecting him to say. "Why didn't you say something?"

"I didn't think it was my place, but Parker kind of told me because of something else I need to confess."

"Well, you're full of confessions today."

He gave her a sheepish grin. "I had asked him to do a background check on your dad, to make sure he was who he said he was. I know I overstepped, but I can't seem to help feeling protective of you. I didn't want anyone else to hurt you."

Tears filled her eyes.

"Oh, hell," he said. "I'm sorry. Can you forgive me?"

She shook her head, and he looked devastated.

"No." She grabbed hold of his hand. "That's not what I mean. It's just...I love you."

She waited, her heart pounding, to see how he would react. But she hadn't been able to hold it in any longer. Slowly, his face transformed in a way that, miracle of miracles, erased her doubt as if it had been drawn on a white-board and then wiped clean.

"I love you, too."

As they ate pizza and talked about their day, Anna felt the power and weight of his gaze upon her. She suspected her gaze might be falling upon him the same way.

After dinner, they cuddled on the couch and watched a movie. She didn't think she'd ever felt better in her life. Having something as simple as the arm of the man she loved around her was indescribably wonderful. She'd missed out on so much because of the belief system on which she was raised.

But she had to acknowledge that it wasn't totally Helena's fault. Anna was proving now that it was possible to break free of indoctrination. She'd just taken the path of least resistance, the one that was less likely to lead to more heartache, until she'd found a person for whom she was willing to take a chance.

She couldn't adequately express how much she loved Roman. Or could she?

As the credits rolled on the movie, she leaned back so that she could look up into Roman's eyes. With her heart going wild again, she asked, "How would you feel if I didn't leave tonight?"

He smiled as he caressed her cheek with a single finger. "I really like that idea. You can stay as long as you want."

The way he kissed her made her believe every word.

Epilogue

ANNA COULDN'T HELP smiling as she waited her turn to give Melody a hug. She'd never seen a more beautiful bride, and the look on Melody's face when she'd stared up at Justin as they exchanged their vows had been something right out of a fairy tale. It was as if Anna was witnessing her own feelings for Roman portrayed by someone else.

"Hey!" Melody said as she saw her and extended her arms for a hug. "You look beautiful."

Anna laughed. "You stole my line."

"Oops."

"Seriously, you look absolutely stunning."

Melody glanced over at her new husband. "It's easy when you're totally in love. Maybe *that's* your secret."

She doubted it was much of a secret how she felt about Roman. Whenever he was around, she couldn't seem to keep a happy grin off her face. But at least he seemed to suffer from the same affliction. Even when he'd been standing next to Justin and Wes as Melody had made her way down the aisle toward her soon-to-be husband, Roman only had eyes for Anna. She had been momentarily glad the wedding was being held outside at the ranch instead of in a church because the thoughts she'd had with his eyes on her had not been church-worthy.

Anna gave way to the other wedding guests wanting to extend their good wishes to the bride and headed for the refreshment table for some punch. She nabbed a couple of petit fours and grabbed a spot at a table to get off her feet. She wasn't used to the strappy heels she was wearing with her new dress.

"Mind if I join you?" Tom McQueen asked.

"Please, do," she said, gesturing toward the white folding chair across from her.

"Where's your other half?"

"Last I saw him, he and Wes were heading around the far end of the house with mischief in their eyes. I suspect Justin's truck is getting a good decorating right about now."

Tom laughed then took a drink of his own punch as he scanned the crowd. "Quite the affair, isn't it?"

"Yeah, everything is just beautiful. And Melody and Justin look so happy."

"They are. I wish his mother was here to see it."

Over the past few months, as she and Roman had grown closer, she'd heard a lot of stories about his mother, things she'd never known about her. It made her realize all the things she'd never experienced with her own mom, and yet it made her miss her more than she had in a long time.

At least her relationship with her father was gradually growing. She'd beaten the odds and been a bone marrow match for him, and he was responding well to treatment. She and Roman had gone to Denver and during that trip met her father's wife and other children. She'd been so nervous she had sworn she was going to throw up, but they had all been nice. And now she had a half-brother and half-sister she was also getting to know.

Add to that the fact that she was giving novel writing another try, and it was amazing how much a person's life could change in less than a year.

When the dancing started a while later, Paige showed up at the table and dragged a blushing Tom onto the portable dance floor, him insisting he was going to smash her toes flat. Anna laughed at her best friend's antics.

"How about we join them?" Roman said next to her ear, sending a delicious shiver down her spine.

Before she could answer, he took her hand and escorted her out to the middle of the dancing crowd.

"Have I told you that you look beautiful today?" he asked.

"Yes, you did. And you look mighty handsome yourself. It's not fair, really. You already look good in cowboy gear and lab coats, and now I have to add suits to the list. You really should have some flaws."

Roman just laughed and spun her around.

After a while, the band paused so that Melody could toss her bouquet. Paige grabbed Anna away from Roman and hurried her to the group of single ladies awaiting the flying flowers. Though it was just a tradition, Anna found that her pulse was rapid as Melody turned her back and flung the bouquet. In the next moment, Anna reached up and it landed in her hands as if she was the intended target. And then as she glanced around and saw that all the other women had stepped away from her, she realized she had been. Melody must have put the word out that she wanted Anna to catch the bouquet.

But then a murmur went through the crowd. Anna noticed several people looking at something behind her, so she turned to see what had drawn their attention.

She gasped at the sight of Roman down on one knee holding open a small black box. She couldn't believe her eyes and met his to see if this was really happening.

"Anna Kenner, ever since you woke up in the hospital I've wanted nothing more than to spend time with you. And that feeling has only grown since I fell in love with you." He paused, taking an obvious breath as if he was nervous. "I want to spend the rest of my life with you. Will you marry me?"

Tears pooled in her eyes. She couldn't believe he was doing this here, now. But there was only one answer she could give.

"Yes."

The entire crowd erupted into applause. Roman got to his feet, slipped the ring onto her shaking finger, and pulled her into his arms. And then he laid one heck of a kiss on her.

"I can't believe you did this at Justin and Melody's wedding. You're stealing their spotlight."

He grinned like a little boy with a secret. "It was Melody's idea. I asked for advice on what would be the most romantic way to propose, and she said this would be when you'd least expect it."

"She was right about that."

"Do you mind that I did it so publicly? I know how shy you can be."

"I'm so happy right now you could have done it on national television and I wouldn't mind."

"Well, let's not go that far."

She laughed, and he kissed her again.

And then they were surrounded by all the people they loved and who loved them back. But their gazes were never far from each other, and she knew before the night ended she'd be back in his arms enjoying yet another kiss from her cowboy—one of many to come as they shared their lives together. As she squeezed his hand, she realized that all the doubt she'd carried about them being together was completely gone and had been for a long time. In its place was the most amazing love she'd ever experienced, the kind that would last a lifetime.

The End

If you enjoyed *A Cowboy's Kiss,*
you'll love the next book in …

The Once Upon a Western Series

Book 1: *Her Cowboy Prince*

Book 2: *A Cowboy's Kiss*

Book 3: *The Cowboy Next Door*

Available now at your favorite online retailer!

Don't miss Trish Milburn's new holiday story...

A Merry Mountain Christmas

Heidi Forrester has it all–a new promotion, great friends, and plans to purchase a condo. But when her Christmas plans don't pan out, she instead vacations solo in Merry, Montana–a picturesque mountain village where it's Christmas year-round. Charmed, she jumps at the chance to join the festivities by assisting the incredibly handsome but understaffed owner of A World of Christmas, a two-story wonderland of Christmas decor, and finds more holiday spirit and fun than she ever did at glamorous resorts.

Ben McNamara can't believe his luck when the beautiful visitor to his store offers to fill his seasonal help vacancy. Even more fortuitous, she's a marketing genius who can help him make A World of Christmas more attractive to potential buyers. But as the date draws close for him to hand off his family's legacy, Ben realizes that maybe it wasn't the ever-present Christmas atmosphere that had bothered him, but rather the fact that he'd never had anyone to share it with.

Can Heidi convince Ben there's so much more to love on Yule Mountain than just Christmas?

About the Author

Trish Milburn is the author of more than 40 novels and novellas in the romance, women's fiction and young adult genres. She's also a two-time winner of Romance Writers of America's prestigious Golden Heart Award, two-time Maggie Award of Excellence winner, and winner of the 2013 EPIC eBook Award for her young adult novel *White Witch*.

She enjoys road trips, traveling by train, and exploring America's National Parks. And though it sounds like a line from a personals ad, she also enjoys walks on the beach – especially since she moved to Florida after growing up in Kentucky and spending 20 years living in Nashville after college. She's a big geek girl, known to cosplay on occasion, channeling characters from Kahlan Amnell (*Legend of the Seeker*) to The Doctor (*Doctor Who*) to a Shadowhunter (The Mortal Instruments series). She loves a good costume/historical drama or sci-fi epic, and if you can combine the two that's even better. That explains why two of her favorite shows of all time are *Firefly* and *Timeless*.

Visit www.trishmilburn.com to learn more about Trish and her books, to sign up for her fun newsletter, and to connect via social media.

Thank you for reading

A Cowboy's Kiss

If you enjoyed this book, you can find more from all our great authors at TulePublishing.com, or from your favorite online retailer.

TULE
PUBLISHING